"I've pror
this sinc

Simon bent toward her, and time stood still as his mouth touched Laura's. His fingers moved over the back of her head, twisting into her hair.

Laura clung to his wide shoulders, her head flung back under the increasingly passionate pressure of his mouth.

When at last he lifted his head, she was shaking. No man had ever made her feel like that. Simon was breathing thickly, his face flushed. "Yes," he said in a husky voice.

"Yes, what?" she asked hesitantly.

"Yes, I like it," Simon said, and moved toward her again.

Laura panicked. "Oh, no, you don't, Mr. Hilliard," she said. "I'm not my sister...."

Maybe Annette could be swayed by Simon Hilliard's doubtful charms, but Laura could not. She was sure of that. Too sure....

CHARLOTTE LAMB
is also the author of these

Harlequin Presents

328—PAGAN ENCOUNTER
334—LOVE IS A FRENZY
339—FRUSTRATION
345—DARK DOMINION
350—FEVER
358—TWIST OF FATE
364—SENSATION
371—STORM CENTRE
374—THE SILKEN TRAP
380—A FROZEN FIRE
387—THE CRUEL FLAME
393—OBSESSION
401—SAVAGE SURRENDER
404—NIGHT MUSIC
412—MAN'S WORLD
417—STRANGER IN THE NIGHT
422—COMPULSION
428—SEDUCTION
435—ABDUCTION

and these

Harlequin Romances

2083—FESTIVAL SUMMER
2103—FLORENTINE SPRING
2161—HAWK IN A BLUE SKY
2181—MASTER OF COMUS
2206—DESERT BARBARIAN

Many of these titles are available at your local bookseller.

For a free catalogue listing all available Harlequin Romances
and Harlequin Presents, send your name and address to:

HARLEQUIN READER SERVICE
1440 South Priest Drive, Tempe, AZ 85281
Canadian address: Stratford, Ontario N5A 6W2

CHARLOTTE LAMB

retribution

Harlequin Books

TORONTO · LONDON · LOS ANGELES · AMSTERDAM
SYDNEY · HAMBURG · PARIS · STOCKHOLM · ATHENS · TOKYO

Harlequin Presents edition published July 1981
ISBN 0-373-10442-1

Original hardcover edition published in 1981
by Mills & Boon Limited

CHAPTER ONE

LAURA had a headache and she was finding it hard to concentrate on her painting this morning. Sunlight was streaming into the studio in what she considered to be an extremely thoughtless fashion. It would have suited her mood better if it had been raining.

Last night had been eventful. She had planned a candlelit dinner for two, but it had turned into a running battle. Stupid of her not to realise that candlelight and wine would give David the idea that he had won his point sooner than he had expected.

Laura had thought better of him. They had only known each other for just over a month. Why did men always try to force the pace? They tried everything from coaxing to blackmail, but they never tried a little patience.

'I'm not jumping into bed with you on the strength of a brief acquaintance,' she had told him, and he had given her a glare of wounded self-esteem as he marched to the door, pulling it open with a gesture meant more as a threat than a serious intention of leaving.

'You want me to go, do you?'

'You know your way out,' Laura had said sweetly, and he had gone red and slammed out of the flat, leaving her to finish the wine and stay up until two a.m. brooding over men's selfishness.

When she was working she became totally absorbed, withdrawn into a world of her own, and the shrill of

the telephone in another room made her jump. Her
hand slipped and a tiny fleck of green shot from the
brush. 'Oh, damn,' she muttered, beginning to remove
it with a careful hand. She ignored the telephone while
she performed this task, shutting out the sound without hesitation. It was one of the signs of her strong-
minded ability to choose and hold a course of action
that she could ignore what would drive most people
mad. Her tenacity was the more fixed for being un-
obtrusive. People often took years to work out that
Laura could not be driven or even coaxed from her
decided path.

When she did answer the phone the voice at the
other end had a staccato irritation. 'I've been ringing
for ten minutes! What were you doing?'

'Hallo, Father,' Laura said calmly. She had realised
long ago that in dealing with her father it was best to
ignore difficult questions. 'How are you?' It was weeks
since she had last spoken to him. George Sloane was
often out of the country and when he was in London
he was usually too busy to waste time on seeing one of
his children.

'Have you seen Annette lately?' George Sloane had
something of Laura's ability to ignore what he felt was
a waste of time. He plunged straight into a topic without delay. His corner-cutting was no doubt very useful
in the business world. Laura stared out of the sitting-
room window and noted the cloudless blue of the June
sky. It seemed a pity to waste time indoors on a day
like this, but she was behind with her book and had a
deadline to keep.

'I saw her on her birthday.'

'When was that?' he asked impatiently.

Laura made a face. 'Three weeks ago.' He might at

least keep track of their birthdays. He only had three children; surely that wasn't too much to ask?

'I can't remember dates,' he said, as though half apologising. 'Did she mention Hilliard then?'

'Who?' Laura watched a large bluebottle which was buzzing around the window trying to get out. Sunlight turned its wings into shimmering transparent silk.

'Simon Hilliard. I've just been talking to her on the phone. I couldn't make her see sense. I talked until I was blue in the face, but she's digging her heels in about him. My God, she's pigheaded!'

Had he only just discovered that? Annette had always been set on her own way. It was a family characteristic which only their brother had escaped, and Laura wasn't sure Philip had been lucky to do so.

Her father sounded furious. He went on, 'If she thinks Hilliard might marry her she's crazy. I don't want her involved with a man like him. He's a notorious woman-chaser. If she's seen around with him her reputation will be nil.'

'Who is he?' Laura asked when he stopped barking out angry words.

'He runs Siltel,' George Sloane told her, as though that made everything clear.

'Siltel,' Laura said slowly, wondering what on earth that was, her blue eyes puzzled. She had heard the name somewhere, but she couldn't place it.

'You must have heard of them—an international computer firm. They started up around seven years ago and have shot ahead. Hilliard's the brains behind them. He's an electronics genius. He worked for me once.' George Sloane had a bitter tang to his voice as he said that, and Laura got the feeling that he regretted ever letting Simon Hilliard go. 'He hates my guts,' he went on. 'We clashed over financing and he walked out. I wouldn't put it past him to be getting his own back over that.'

'Surely not?' Laura said automatically. That was how her father thought, of course. He was more than capable of taking a revenge by using personal relations to hurt someone, but Laura found it hard to believe that other people were prepared to use such methods.

'Typical of Annette to get mixed up with him. Look here, Laura, you've got to see her, talk some sense into her.'

Laura put a hand to her forehead and smoothed out the lines which had wrinkled it as he spoke. 'I doubt if she'd listen to me.'

Annette never listened to anybody. She was beautiful, silly and spoilt, and for two of those things their father was responsible. Annette was the only one of his children in whom he had ever shown what amounted to a personal interest. He had been proud of her looks as a child and had boasted about her to his friends and business acquaintances, showered her with presents, made a great fuss of her. It had given Annette an inflated idea of her own importance. Laura had never managed to make her sister listen to a word she said.

'You must make her listen!'

'That's easier said than done,' Laura pointed out.

'Hilliard has invited her to go to Paris with him,' George Sloane barked. 'There's an international conference due in a couple of weeks and Siltel will be represented. That swine had the nerve to ask her to go with him—my daughter! I'd like to get my hands round his neck!'

'Did Annette tell you that?' Laura was surprised. She hadn't thought Annette would confide such news to her father.

'No, Donald did.'

'How did Donald know?'

'The girl who shares her flat—what's her name?'

'Lucy,' said Laura.

'Well, she told Donald, warned him what Annette was planning.'

'That's nice of Lucy,' Laura said drily. 'I wonder why she did that.'

George Sloane brushed that aspect aside. 'I told Annette she wasn't even to consider going, and all she did was laugh and tell me she was a big girl now.' He breathed heavily. 'I thought it was settled that she was going to marry Donald. He's perfect for her. How can she be so stupid as to get mixed up with a man like Hilliard?'

Laura doubted if Annette had paused to consider the possible consequences. Annette was used to having Donald on a string and she had never allowed her relationship with him to get in the way of other, temporary, flings. She took the view that she had the right to enjoy herself while she was young and Donald wasn't interfering with her fun.

'I'm relying on you to get her back in line,' George Sloane informed Laura, who made a face at his peremptory tone.

She managed to keep the resentment out of her voice. 'Well, I'll talk to her, but I can't promise she'll listen.' Not if she knew Annette.

'She'd better. 'Bye.' George Sloane hung up without wasting time on further courtesy, and Laura replaced her own receiver more slowly, frowning.

Did he really believe Annette would listen to her? Had he already tried Philip and had no luck? Annette would hardly listen to Philip, either. Philip was the most biddable of them. He had obediently entered the family firm at the age of twenty-one, on leaving college, and had slowly climbed the ladder in the firm at his father's dictate. He was now in quite a high executive position, but was still very much a pale shadow of his father. He had even married the girl George Sloane picked out for him. It had all the appearance of being a fairly happy marriage, Laura had to grant that. Daphne was quite good-looking, slim and pleasant in feature if rather lifeless. She never put a foot wrong or said a word out of place. She dressed in excellent taste and gave beautifully arranged dinner parties for the right people. Laura sometimes suspected George Sloane had had her run up to size. If Philip found her wanting in any way he never gave a sign of it.

Annette did not like Daphne and made no bones about it. She was scornful of her brother for having married to order. Annette knew, of course, that her father wished to see her married to Donald. 'He can think again,' she had said, her face very flushed. 'I'll choose my own guy.'

Laura glanced down at her jeans and blue shirt. Should she change before going round to Annette's flat? It might look more casual if she just dropped in on the offchance.

Laura's flat was on the ground floor of a rambling old Victorian house which lay on the far side of Hampstead Heath looking down towards Golders Green. She had inherited some money from her maternal grandfather when she was twenty-one and had bought the flat in order to be entirely independent from her father. She earned enough from her children's books to be able to keep herself comfortably if she was careful with the money.

She had recognised early on that George Sloane used money as a weapon and a trap. Both Philip and Annette had accepted his help without noticing the strings he tied to it. Annette might be rebelling now, but Laura knew that it was their father who paid the rent of Annette's flat, bought her clothes with a monthly allowance, made it possible for her to live quite luxuriously on the tiny salary she earned as a trainee vendeuse for a London fashion house.

Annette would, in the end, have the choice of coming to heel or losing the standard of living she enjoyed so much. She was wildly extravagant. She took taxis without thinking about it, bought perfume and cosmetics by the shoal and lived in a permanent whirl of social excitement.

George Sloane was using Laura at this juncture because he wanted to avoid a head-on clash with Annette unless he had to, but if he felt it was necessary he would ruthlessly apply the screws as far as money was concerned. That would come later when he had tried other methods.

Laura took a wicker shopping basket and let herself out of her flat. As she walked across the Heath and down the hill into Hampstead Village her eyes restlessly skimmed the traffic, her mind set on the subject of her sister.

On the way to Annette's flat she did some shopping to give herself an excuse and when Annette opened the door to her she was groaning under the weight of her basket.

'Can I beg a cup of coffee? I'm dead!'

'Oh, hi,'. Annette said without enthusiasm. They had never been very close. The six years between them had been too big a gap to be bridged, somehow.

Annette did not even look like Laura. She was tall for a girl, her figure perfectly proportioned, her hair a flame of red-gold which she wore in a tossing cloud around her face. She glanced over her shoulder into her flat now, making a grimace.

'It's a bit of a mess. I'm having a party tonight and I'm in the throes.'

'A party?' Laura supported her heavy basket with her hip. 'Why wasn't I invited?'

'Didn't I mention it? I thought you knew. Of course you're invited.' Annette didn't sound wildly keen, though.

'Look, can I come in or not?' Laura asked mildly. 'My arm is almost breaking.'

Annette reluctantly stepped back. 'Sure. Park the basket and make yourself some coffee. I must tidy the flat before tonight.'

Annette saw no reason why she should pretend hospitable enthusiasm for a mere sister and Laura did not press the point. She went into the flat and put down her basket. The sitting-room looked as though a bomb had hit it. Chairs and floor were strewn with records and clothes.

'My God!' Laura exclaimed.

'I'm just tidying up,' Annette said defensively.

'When I've had my coffee I'll join you,' Laura promised, going into the minute kitchenette.

Annette followed. 'Oh, you are a pet. I don't know where to start.'

Laura could believe it. She wondered where to start herself. The flat probably needed to be worked on for hours. She made the coffee while Annette draped herself elegantly over a chair, running a long hand through her cloudy hair while she talked.

'Is Donald coming to the party?' Laura asked innocently.

'Do me a favour,' Annette said with disgust. 'You might as well ask if Daddy's coming.'

'Is he?'

Annette eyed her with scorn. 'Of course not. Nor is Donald, believe me.'

'Is Donald out of favour?'

'He was never in.'

Laura lifted her brows without saying anything.

'Daddy just thinks he was,' Annette broke out as though she had said something.

Laura nodded calmly, passing her some coffee. She perched on a high green kitchen stool rather uncomfortably and sipped her own coffee.

Annette lowered her artificial lashes and gave Laura a secretive look through them. 'You coming, then?' she asked, and there was a faintly wary tone in her voice now.

'Love to,' Laura said cheerfully. 'I'll bring a bottle, shall I?'

Annette bit her little finger, her brow crinkling. 'Seen Daddy lately?'

'Not for months.' That was true. His call this morning was the first she had heard from him since the New Year when he had rung her from Tokyo in an alcoholic moment of nostalgia, only to have nothing much to say when it came to it.

'Seen Donald?'

'I never see Donald,' said Laura. 'Except in the papers when he's quoted on some matter of international finance, and I never read a word of that.'

'He's a dead bore,' Annette said.

'I rather like his ears,' Laura murmured.

Annette lifted her head and gazed in wild surmise.

'They're pointed, haven't you ever noticed? When he's middle-aged he'll go bald and then he'll look like a little green man from Mars.'

Annette giggled. 'You're right—I never noticed.'

'I'm paid to notice things like that,' Laura pointed out.

Annette looked down into her coffee. 'There'll be someone special at the party.'

'Oh?' Laura glanced at her watch. 'Hurry up with the coffee and we'll tackle your flat before I go.'

She knew better than to betray interest. That would scare Annette off at once.

Annette bristled. 'Plenty of time. I'm glad you'll be there. You'll like Simon.'

'Simon?'

'Hilliard,' said Annette. 'He's fantastic.'

'Your latest guy? They always are.' Laura drank some more of her coffee. 'I never knew anyone go through so many men so fast.'

Annette looked flattered, preening on her chair with bright eyes. Laura thought of a parrot in London Zoo who looked just like that when you said: who's a pretty boy?

'He's different. Simon is special.' Catching Laura's disbelieving smile, she insisted: 'He is.'

'If you say so.'

'You wait until you meet him. You'll be bowled over.'

'I hope not,' Laura said gravely.

Annette stared at her. 'What?'

'You wouldn't want me to fall for your man, would you?'

Annette giggled, tossing back her hair. She had a series of little gestures which she made with conscious grace. Some of them she based on the models at her fashion house, others she had worked out for herself.

'It wouldn't do you any good if you did. He's crazy about me.'

Laura's face didn't alter, but she studied her sister with inner concern. There had been a breathless excitement in the way Annette said that which bothered Laura. Until now, it had always been the men chasing Annette, not the other way around. Laura became very intent.

'What does Lucy think of him?' she asked casually. Lucy Allan shared the flat with Annette and Laura respected her judgment. Lucy was several years older than Annette and very level-headed. She was engaged to an airline pilot who had never stayed on the ground long enough to get married. Lucy was wryly understanding of him. 'I'll catch him between flights one day,' she said when the question of a marriage date came up.

'Oh, Lucy,' Annette said, shrugging one shoulder.

'She doesn't like him?'

'She says he's very sexy,' Annette offered evasively.

'But she isn't keen?'

Annette looked irritated. That had not been the right response. 'What does Lucy know? She can't even get that Geoffrey guy to stay still long enough to marry her.'

Laura finished her coffee and stood up. 'Shall we get your flat knocked into shape, then?'

It took around an hour and when it was done Annette was lying on the long green studio couch in an attitude of exhaustion brought on apparently by watching Laura work so hard.

Laura stood eyeing her with wry amusement. 'I hope you aren't too knocked out to enjoy your party. How about the food? Is that all laid on?'

'Crisps and peanuts,' said Annette. 'I'm not a millionaire.'

'And the drinks?'

'Bring a bottle. Everyone knows that.'

'I see.' Laura did see. 'It's going to be a makeshift party, is it?'

'Simon promised to bring plenty of whisky.'

'Generous guy,' Laura murmured. From what her father had said, Simon Hilliard could afford it.

'He's super.' Annette managed to raise some enthusiasm with that remark. 'Wait till you see him.' She bit her lower lip for a moment, her teeth small and white and even. 'I'm going to Paris with him,' she flung defiantly, staring at Laura and waiting for the reaction.

'I hope the weather stays nice for you,' said Laura, picking up her basket and moving to the door. 'Make sure you get at least a bottle of Patou out of it. A weekend in Paris ought to rate that.'

Annette's face ran with hot colour. 'That's not very nice,' she said in a childishly aggrieved voice.

Laura looked over her shoulder with bland amusement. 'Oh, isn't it that sort of trip to Paris? Sorry. I've just remembered where I heard of him before and I thought it must be.'

'What do you mean? What have you heard? Donald *has* been talking to you.' Annette was instantly up from the couch and burning with temper, her cheeks bright red.

'I haven't spoken to him for months. No, I've just

heard a few things about Simon Hilliard and his women.'

'Oh, newspapers,' Annette dismissed. 'Lies, all of it.'

Laura smiled. 'Of course,' she said smoothly, opening the door.

'They are,' Annette insisted, pursuing her.

'I believe you,' Laura agreed in the tone of someone who doesn't believe a word.

'What do you think I am? A Victorian maiden? Why shouldn't I go to Paris with him?'

'No reason on earth,' Laura said reasonably. 'What you do with your life is up to you, darling. Personally I wouldn't want to be classed with the sort of easy lady Simon Hilliard picks up and drops after a few weeks, but maybe you want to be known as a pushover.'

She walked out of the front door while Annette stood there, gasping like a landed fish, and was out of earshot before her sister had thought of a few stinging retorts.

Laura had some idea of her sister's character. Annette might be fond of the high life, she might be empty-headed, but she was made of the same basic stuff as their father. She had a rock-bottom desire to be safe which Laura had noticed more than once during their shared childhood. Annette disliked taking risks. She also had a high opinion of herself, and she wouldn't want to have people laughing at her behind her back. If she thought Simon Hilliard would treat her the way he had treated other women she would be very wary of him. The problem was that her vanity would make her believe that Simon Hilliard was genuinely in love with her.

Clashing head-on with her as their father had done

would merely make her obstinate. What Laura had to do was to make Annette think, and she wouldn't do that if Annette imagined that Laura was making conventional noises at her.

It was possible, of course, that her father had it wrong. Simon Hilliard might have fallen for Annette. Laura had automatically accepted her father's view of the matter, but she hadn't failed to notice that he had a biased opinion of Simon Hilliard.

As she got ready for the party that evening the phone rang. She was brushing her hair in front of her mirror and made a little face at herself as the ringing began. What was the betting that that was her father again checking to see if she had sorted Annette out yet?

It wasn't. For a second or two she didn't place the quiet, careful voice, then she said: 'Donald?'

'How are you, Laura?' Donald Foulds always went through the conventional paths of conversation. He did everything by the book.

'Very well. And you?' Laura accepted his lead. It only threw him off his course to make anything but an equally conventional response.

'Fine,' he said flatly. 'Work going well?' That was one point in Donald's favour. He took her children's books as seriously as her publisher and without the incentive of making money from them. He had even bought some of them to give to a niece who lived in Scotland.

'Fine. How's the bank?'

Donald permitted himself a small joke. 'We aren't losing money.'

'I bet,' said Laura, and he laughed.

After a pause to show that he was coming to the

point of his call he asked: 'Seen Annette lately?'

'I'm just off to her party,' Laura told him.

'I heard she was having one,' Donald admitted. He paused again, then in a sheepish tone asked her: 'May I ask if you're . . . er . . . going with anyone?'

Laura could see the next question coming a mile off and she made a face at herself in the mirror. 'Well, no.'

'I suppose you wouldn't object if I took you?' Donald laughed deprecatingly and she felt angry with him.

Annette hadn't invited him, wouldn't want him, but what could Laura say? She paused just long enough to recognise that she hadn't got a shred of an excuse for refusing and said: 'How nice of you.'

Donald sighed with relief. 'The thing is,' he confided, lowering his tone as though the phone was bugged, 'Annette and I aren't on very good terms at the moment. She's running around with some chap I don't much care for and she's being very difficult.'

'Won't she think it odd if I turn up with you in tow?' Laura pointed out.

Donald considered that for a moment. 'We've known each other for years,' he said brightly. 'Why shouldn't we go to parties together?'

'Why shouldn't we?' said Laura, wondering if he was quite right in the head. Annette would leap to a lot of conclusions, most of them absolutely spot on. I really ought to tell Donald a few home truths, she thought. He ought to realise that by running after Annette so blatantly he's only sending her in the opposite direction fast, but I can't run everybody's life for them. All I want is a quiet life of my own. I don't want to turn into an agony column overnight.

'Pick me up in an hour,' she said. 'And Donald—bring a bottle.'

'Of what?' he asked earnestly.

'Choose your own poison,' Laura murmured. 'Whisky, gin, lemonade.'

He brought all three. She might have known, Laura thought as he displayed them proudly, that he had no sense of humour whatever. 'Oh, fantastic,' she said, though, scrutinising his idea of party gear with disbelief. The suit was beautifully tailored, but she had a shrewd idea it would look very out of place at Annette's idea of a party.

Donald was in his late thirties. You couldn't call him handsome, but he had a face which was easy to like. There was something oddly comical about it when he was not being serious and when he was his sober look made one laugh even more. His face was thin, very smooth, his eyes diffident and a pale grey. His brown hair was thinning slightly and one could see just what he would look like when he was bald.

She wondered what on earth he saw in Annette, apart from the obvious. What did he imagine they would talk about? They were light years apart. Laura couldn't imagine her sister married to him. Annette would twist him round her little finger and probably make him miserable, but perhaps Donald saw their possible future together as nothing but bliss.

Poor Donald, she thought, watching him driving through the crowded Saturday streets on their way to Annette's flat. He was in for a shock if his dreams came true.

He cleared his throat in preparation for some major statement and shot her a look. 'Has she mentioned Hilliard to you yet?'

'The name came up,' Laura admitted guardedly.

His cheeks flushed. 'He doesn't have a reputation for staying faithful. Annette doesn't know what she's doing.'

Laura suspected Annette knew only too well, or thought she did. She watched Donald's unassertive face thoughtfully.

'What's he like?'

'Clever,' said Donald, at once thinking of him in business terms. 'He's red-hot where exports are concerned. His export lines have grown steadily over the past three years . . .'

'Donald, as a man.'

'Oh,' said Donald, frowning. 'As I said—his reputation isn't exactly pretty.'

'Where women are concerned?'

'He never keeps them for long,' Donald said in a dry voice. 'I'm worried about Annette. She's so young. She's blinded by his looks.'

Laura glanced at his pointed ears. 'You're very sweet, Donald.'

His ears went pink. 'Thank you,' he said angrily.

'I wasn't being sarcastic.'

'No, only patronising.'

Laura looked at him in surprise. 'Sorry.'

'I'm not a fool, you know. I realise I'm too old for her, but she needs someone who understands her and can look after her.'

'So she does,' Laura said slowly. 'But barging into the party with me isn't the way. Unless . . .'

'Unless?' he picked up at once, hopefully.

'Unless she thinks I've snaffled you for myself.'

Donald looked alarmed, shifting in his seat as though edging away from her. He was a very wealthy man and no doubt women had tried for him in the past. He gave Laura a cagey look, and she began to laugh.

'No, Donald dear, I'm not on your trail. You're a nice man, but I haven't got any intentions where you're concerned.'

Rather red, he muttered: 'Good Lord, I didn't think you had.'

'I was just thinking aloud. How would it be if we gave Annette the idea that I did have intentions, though?'

Donald didn't like it. 'Well, I don't think . . .'

'Annette has a streak of dog-in-the-manger about her,' Laura went on, and Donald looked furious.

'Well, thank you! You mean she would only want me if she thought someone else wanted me first?'

'I'm being very clumsy tonight,' Laura apologised. 'Don't get sensitive, Donald, there's a sweet man. By all means walk in there tonight and make no bones about your reason for being there, but don't be surprised if Annette sends you packing with a flea in your ear.'

Donald looked gloomily at the windscreen. 'I see what you mean.'

Laura sighed. 'Well, I'm glad about that.'

'What do you suggest?'

She shrugged. 'Just stick with me like glue and look amorous if you can manage it.'

'My God!' Donald muttered.

'I said, if you can manage it.'

He groaned. 'I'll try.'

'Not too amorous,' Laura added warily.

Donald laughed and she looked at him in surprise again. 'I shan't go too far,' he promised, and she wondered if he had more of a sense of humour than she had imagined.

As Laura had expected, Annette looked deeply suspicious as soon as she set eyes on Donald. Laura had grabbed his hand as the door opened and she beamed at her sister, pretending not to notice the sharp little green eyes.

'Hi, we brought a few bottles.'

'What's he doing here?' Annette demanded.

'Donald and I had dinner together,' said Laura, looking at her with sweet innocence, 'so I brought him with me. You look very smart, doesn't she, Donald?'

Annette looked more than smart. She was wearing crushed velvet trousers which had apparently been moulded to her and a very low-cut black silk shirt. She looked vivid and elated, her eyes very bright, her hair a floating red cloud.

Donald gave her a brief look. 'Fantastic,' he agreed, looking back down at Laura. 'So do you, but I've told you that already.'

Laura looked demurely at him. 'I don't mind if you repeat yourself.'

'Good, because I'm going to,' he said, and she was very impressed by his acting ability. She wondered, indeed, if he had sampled some of his own whisky before coming out. He had a distinct flush already.

Annette looked from one to the other of them sharply. Someone in the crowded sitting-room yelled for her at that moment and she turned away. Laura dragged Donald past her into the scrum. Lucy was at the other side of the room, helping someone mix drinks, and she gave them a relieved beam when they handed over their bottles.

'That's great, we were running low.' Lucy was a

secretary with one of the major airlines. Slim, calm and level-headed, she was a surprising choice of friend for Annette, but opposites often seemed to be drawn to each other and Lucy found Annette's lively personality amusing. Laura had hoped at one time that Lucy's common sense would rub off on Annette, but it showed no sign of doing so. At times Lucy became very irritated with Annette and Laura could not help speculating that Lucy was slightly jealous of Annette's success with the men she met.

'How's your man?' Laura asked her smilingly now.

'Stopping over in Rio,' Lucy said bitterly. 'He should be home for two minutes, next Wednesday. Big deal.' She looked at Donald with disapproving eyes. 'If you had any sense you wouldn't be here. Why don't you just forget her?'

'I have,' Donald said exuberantly, sliding an arm around Laura's waist.

Lucy looked staggered. 'Oh,' she said. 'Sorry.' She gave Laura a long, surprised stare. 'Well, have a good time.'

'We will,' Donald assured her, picking up a glass of whisky and swallowing it while the two girls watched him.

'Let's dance,' he said, putting down the empty glass.

Laura felt like someone who has let a genie out of his bottle. 'Don't overdo it, will you?' she whispered in his ear as they moved away.

'I'm a bit fed up,' he announced in self-excuse. 'I really feel like chucking myself in the Thames.'

'You poor man,' said Laura, suppressing a smile.

'You can't ever have been in love, or you wouldn't be so unsympathetic!'

'Hell, is it?' Laura couldn't take his love seriously,

somehow. His face was too amusing. It made him difficult to take seriously.

'Don't laugh!'

'I'm sorry,' she said, trying not to without much success. Donald was dancing beside her in an ungainly attempt to mimic her graceful movements, his limbs stiff and uneasy. He gave her a sulky little stare.

Laura was a slender, fine-boned girl with long blonde hair and a perfectly proportioned face. Her nose was small and straight, her blue eyes widely spaced, her mouth a warm pink curve which could straighten into determination in a certain mood. She had a deceptive air of fragility which made men feel protective until they discovered the tough inner core which her apparent delicacy hid. They seemed to take it as a personal insult that Laura was not the pliable, yielding creature her looks suggested.

Her clear eyes and calm voice could carry the faintest trace of amusement, which made some men feel uncomfortable. They were never sure if she was laughing at them, but they were afraid she might be, and they didn't like it. A man trying to talk someone into bed doesn't enjoy being laughed at, in Laura's experience. It had always worked in the past when someone was getting rather too pressing. Passion withered before her amused blue eyes.

Laura had grown up in house where emotion was suspect. Her mother had always been very withdrawn, her father curt and indifferent, so Laura had learnt to inhibit her own reactions to those around her, watching them from distance. She saw people with cool, reasoning, amused clarity, and the men she had met so far seemed to resent that attitude.

Her classic blonde looks increased that suggestion of

coldness. Her sense of humour lay below the surface, revealing itself in flashes in the blue eyes, a faint suppressed quiver of the mouth. The emotional vacuum which her childhood had produced had never been filled. Laura had never been within a mile of falling in love. She kept life at a safe distance. Falling in love seemed to her from what she had observed of it in others a ridiculous and painful process, and so far she had avoided any threat of it.

Looking at Donald she pondered on the lunacy of his feelings for her sister. It was no coincidence that the Greeks had chosen to make the god of love a blindfolded, irresponsible child. Love had a crazy irrationality which took no heed of how and where it struck.

'I don't care what anyone thinks,' Donald said irrelevantly.

Or was it irrelevant? Laura thought, giving him a soothing smile. Donald was in love and he was gloomily defying the world's judgment.

'She's so beautiful,' he groaned, staring over her shoulder. 'That's him with her now, the swine.'

Laura shifted so that she could see her sister. Annette was also dancing, her face as lit up as an electric bulb. Her partner was looking down at her and as Laura considered him she felt a spasm of uneasiness.

Whatever she had been expecting from what she had heard of him, Simon Hilliard was a surprise. In profile his face had a darkly handsome stamp which did not have the sort of self-indulgent weakness she had imagined she would see. His nose was straight and chiselled, his jawline determined. There was no flaw in the physical structure of his face to give her a clue how to deal with him.

He suddenly laughed at something Annette had

said, lifting his head, so that his eyes became visible, their heavy lids drawn back. Green, mocking, they had dark pupils rayed with tiny threads of yellow which deepened their colour. Laura was reminded of a cat, but no domestic cat—a sleek, dangerous animal, moving with lazy grace as it closed in for the kill.

Annette was gazing up at him, hypnotised, judging from her rapt expression, and he was looking back at her with the satisfied smile of the tiger.

CHAPTER TWO

'WHAT do you think of him?' Donald asked in her ear, his voice glum.

'I'll reserve judgment.'

'I'd like to smash his face in,' Donald announced with surprising belligerence. He had grown even more flushed and the dancing was making him breathe heavily. The whisky, or emotion? Laura thought, considering him with concern.

'Shall we sit down for a while?' she suggested. She didn't want Donald collapsing in an abject heap under Annette's amused, contemptuous gaze. Also his dancing left much to be desired and Laura was aware of getting some grins from the people around them as he weaved about like a drunken elephant. He had no sense of rhythm and no elasticity in his body.

'Sit where?' he asked gloomily, staring round the overcrowded room.

'Well, let's prop up the wall for a bit,' Laura advised cheerfully, pulling him out of the general scrum which took up most of the space. She knew some of the other guests by sight, if not always by name, and they were soon deep in talk with a group of people discussing a new play which had opened in London that week. Donald barely made a pretence of listening, his eyes straying towards Annette every two seconds.

Annette had also stopped dancing. She was the centre of attention on the other side of the room, laughing and talking in a circle of amused faces. Simon Hilliard was one of them for a while, but then he wandered away, his black brows slanting in cool amusement. Somehow he gave Laura the impression of a strange animal in alien territory: not quite at home with his surroundings and watchful of those around him. Laura saw him join some girls, speak to them, heard them laughing.

'That music's very loud,' Donald muttered. It was heavy weather making conversation with him. He thought in well-trodden paths, never wandering far from what he felt was expected of him. She got the feeling he was lost without some sort of guideline about what to say.

'Heavy rock,' Laura agreed. The crash of the insistent beat made the walls seem to waver, but the dancers didn't seem to notice. Maybe their ears were accustomed to it.

Donald looked at her, a glass in his hand, his flush growing more pronounced. 'That's a pretty outfit,' he commented.

'Thank you,' Laura murmured gravely, hoping he wasn't going to get absolutely drunk. She did not feel up to coping with a man in that condition.

'You're really very pretty, Laura,' Donald announced in an aggressive, assertive voice. 'Very pretty.'

'Thank you,' she said with amusement. Yes, he was going to turn difficult, she sensed. At the moment he was just teetering on the brink of it, but if he drank much more he would go right over the edge.

Annette materialised beside them, eyeing her sister without favour. 'Enjoying yourselves?'

The question had a bite to it, but Laura smiled

sweetly at her. 'Yes, fabulous party. We're having a great time.'

'Yes, fabulous,' Donald echoed, trying hard to sound as though he meant it.

Annette gave him a come-hither look from under her lashes. 'You haven't danced with me all evening, Donny.'

He went pink, staring at her with mesmerised fascination as she fluttered her lashes at him. Annette performed one of her favourite little tricks, her head tilted back, a half-smile curving her pink mouth, one hand thrusting back her full, cloudy red hair.

'Dance with me now,' she pouted.

To do him justice Donald made a valiant attempt at resistance. He stood stock still, muttering: 'Oh—er—well . . .'

Annette curved an arm around his neck and drew him towards her, her curved body melting against him, gazing all the time into his saucer eyes. His neck went brick red.

Was that it? Laura pondered. Was it Annette's obvious and uninhibited manner which attracted Donald? He was himself so shy and cautious, so tightly locked up inside his careful upbringing, that someone like Annette flattened him and left him reeling. He was attracted by the very opposite of himself. Perhaps he wished he could behave with such untrammelled indifference to any social code. Donald was the quiet introvert pulled by magnetic drag to the extrovert and unable to break free because deep inside his head he didn't want to.

'Don't you want to dance with me?' Annette coaxed, fixing him with snakelike intention.

Donald gulped and gave Laura a despairing look.

She decided to let him down, since he apparently couldn't save himself.

'Don't mind me,' she said.

'Don't mind her,' Annette agreed with faintly vicious sweetness, dragging him away.

Donald was torn, it seemed to Laura, between elation at having Annette show him so much interest at last and a desire to prove to her that he wasn't entirely in her pocket, the shift of these contradictory emotions making his face even more comic.

Laura wandered off to get herself a drink. 'Well, that didn't last long, did it?' Lucy pointed out, giving her a pitying smile. 'I could have told you Annette would grab him back as soon as she spotted what was going on—you should know by now that she hates to let anything go.'

'Sad, isn't it?' Laura asked cheerfully, turning away. Some friends of her own had just arrived and were talking on the other side of the room. She squeezed past a knot of people to get to them, but someone stepped back right into her and her glass lurched, sending gin and orange splashing down her black velvet skirt.

'Oh, damn!' Laura exclaimed involuntarily.

'Sorry, clumsy of me,' the man apologised, going down on his knees to inspect the damage and whipping out a handkerchief to carry out mopping-up operations before the gin soaked into the material.

Laura regarded the top of the black head with ironic disbelief. He stood up, smiling at her. 'Okay, no permanent damage done,' he promised, his face altering slightly as he observed her.

Laura studied him calmly and openly. Tall and lean-hipped, he was wearing a black shirt and black jeans which streamlined his long body and enforced

the impact of that handsome face, drawing the eye
to it. His hair had a springy vitality and was faintly
dishevelled. Laura could remember watching Annette
running her fingers caressingly through it as they
danced.

'We haven't met, have we?' he asked, beginning to
look amused by her prolonged inspection of him. 'I'd
remember if we had.'

Laura absorbed the flattery of that without reaction. She was aware that she would remember him,
too. He wasn't a man one would lightly forget. She
could understand why Annette hung round him like
bindweed.

'I'm Simon,' he informed her, skating another
glance from the smooth blonde hair framing her face,
to her feet, lingering en route to appreciate the scenery
in a faintly teasing fashion which he underlined by
grinning at her as he looked back at her face.

Laura resisted the temptation to let herself like him.
'I know,' she said.

He registered the cool tone and lifted one of those
fine, dark brows. 'Have I had a bad press? It isn't true,
lies all of it. I'm very nice to know.'

'I'll remember that,' Laura promised, half turning.

He caught her arm, his long fingers curling round it
in a grip which, without being painful, did not mean
to let go. 'Hey, where are you going? You haven't even
told me your name or left your slipper so that I can go
out with a town-crier to find out who you are.' The
green eyes mocked, laughing, and Laura surveyed him
thoughtfully.

'Oh, you won't need a town-crier,' she assured him.
'Annette will fill you in with all the details.' If she
hadn't heard anything about him she would have

summed him up pretty accurately from the intimate, teasing charm of those green eyes. He was very sure of himself, sure of the effect he could have with that quick smile.

'Annette is a friend of yours?' She caught the flicker of speculation in his eyes before he veiled them with thick black lashes. 'Are you one of the models from her place?' The lashes shifted and he viewed her again, estimating the slight but feminine curve of her body. 'You're skinny enough, but are you tall enough, I wonder? On the other hand, you do have the right haughty manner, I suppose.'

Laura smiled without amusement. 'You used to work for my father, I believe?' she said, deliberately taking the attack.

His eyes narrowed, the black brows slanted. Moving closer, he stared at her hard. 'You're Laura Sloane,' he said slowly. 'I see,' spinning out the words as though to cover whatever was going on inside his black head.

'I gather you didn't get on with my father,' Laura said in a conventionally polite voice which didn't quite hide her antagonism.

His mouth twisted. 'He told you that, did he? Did he tell you why? He skimps on research and is too damned mean to take proper safety precautions in the factories. The accident rate was dangerously high.'

'I'm not involved in the way my father runs his business,' Laura told him. She could believe that Simon Hilliard was absolutely right in his accusations, but her father never discussed business with her.

'And you don't care?' he asked curtly, that give-away slant of his brows holding distinct contempt. 'So long as the books keep showing a profit it doesn't matter?'

'The profitability or otherwise of my father's company is nothing to do with me.'

'You just pay your allowance into the bank and sleep well at night?'

'I don't get an allowance.' Laura felt a flash of temper go through her as she snapped back.

'You don't?' He made that a polite note of disbelief.

'That's nothing to do with you, though,' Laura told him with a sting in her voice.

'I get the feeling you're a chip off the old block,' he said, and he did not intend that to flatter her. 'You're very different from your sister, aren't you?'

'Thank you,' Laura said gravely, back under control now and refusing to let him get to her again.

There was an odd glow in the green eyes for a second. Laura caught it briefly before he glanced down and wondered if she was wrong in thinking that she had seen rage in them.

'I gather your father disapproves of Annette seeing me,' he remarked, watching her through those long lashes.

'I don't think he's crazy about the idea.'

'He prefers Foulds. Of course Foulds is the safe type.' He pretended to consider the idea, his head to one side. 'The marrying type,' he concluded mockingly.

'And you're not?'

He laughed, cynicism in the flash of his eyes. 'Oh, I'm not. I'm glad you noticed. Did she tell you she was coming to Paris with me?'

That was carrying the war into the enemy's camp with a vengeance, Laura realised. She met the mocking green eyes head on and her face was icy. 'She told me.'

'And you said?' Under the smile in those bright eyes was that glowing expression and now she was certain it was rage.

'Ask her,' Laura suggested.

'I will,' he promised. 'I get the feeling you disapprove. She's of age. If she chooses to come to Paris with me that's her affair, surely?'

'You took the words right out of my mouth,' Laura said crisply.

His face hardened although he kept that mocking little smile. 'She'll come, you know,' he said.

'Will she?' Laura had to struggle to keep her face and voice unrevealing, neutral, but inwardly she was beginning to feel very angry. She had very little evidence to go on, but she had picked up a hostility in him which had only appeared once he knew who she was, and that was revealing. What had he quarrelled with her father about? He talked of problems about the management of the firm, but she had a shrewd idea there was something more personal than that behind it all. Simon Hilliard disliked her father, and it was mutual. Why?

'Yes, she will,' he drawled, watching her.

'I shouldn't bet on it,' Laura snapped.

'Oh, well, if we're laying bets,' he said at once, the green eyes glinting. 'What do you offer? What's the stake?'

Her colour rose. 'Very funny!'

'I wasn't being funny. It was your suggestion.'

'You shouldn't pick up casual phrases! You must know I didn't mean it.'

'Women never mean anything, they must talk without stopping to think what they're saying.'

'I wouldn't dream of laying bets on whether or not

you could seduce my sister,' Laura bit back, surprised to realise that her temper had slipped again. He was getting under her skin and she didn't like it.

'What makes you think I haven't?' he enquired lazily.

Laura pulled herself back from the verge of open rage and said with deliberation: 'She wouldn't be so defiant about going to Paris if you had.'

He stared down at her, his expression speculative. 'Now that's shrewd. You're right, she wouldn't. And I haven't.' He paused and said softly: 'But I will.'

Laura stiffened, giving him a straight, contemptuous stare. 'I suppose you think that's funny?'

'Hardly the word I'd choose,' he drawled.

Laura had a lot of other words seething on the tip of her tongue, but anger jammed them together and she stared at him, speechless.

'Go on,' he encouraged, leaning beside her in a relaxed and casual way which spoke of enjoyment. She just looked at him and he grinned. 'I can read your mind, you know,' he told her.

'Then that saves me the trouble of telling you what I think of you,' Laura flashed.

'Go ahead,' he urged. 'Like most people I love to hear myself talked about.'

'You're a very conceited man, Mr Hilliard!'

If she had hoped to prick his skin with a remark like that she was wrong. He just grinned at her again. 'You have a very attractive voice, has anyone ever told you that?'

The personal remark threw her, and she looked away. She had the distinct impression that that was why he had made it. He was digging away at her, watching every flicker of expression passing over her face.

'Very cool and level,' he went on. 'It matches your looks. You're a very cool lady altogether, aren't you? On the surface, anyway.'

'Am I supposed to find that flattering?' Laura asked, turning to meet his eyes.

'It was just a statement of fact. In your own way, you're as stunning as your sister, but I'd never have guessed you were related. You're far more of a challenge.'

'Is that what women are, to you? A challenge?'

'Oh, they have their place in my life,' he assured her with a wicked mockery in his green eyes. 'I'll admit I soon get bored, though. I find women have a short-term entertainment value.'

It fitted what she had heard about him. She watched him, her face cool. 'And when you're bored?'

'I give them a kiss and push them out of the door,' he admitted, smiling. 'I'm a busy man. My work takes up most of my energy.'

The black pupils had a hard, assured gleam as he gazed back at her. It was easy to see why he had managed to capture and fascinate Annette. Annette's easy victories over other men would make her eager to add Simon Hilliard to their number.

'You may be the human equivalent of a computer,' Laura told him coldly, 'but Annette is still very young and she could get hurt.'

His brows lifted in a sardonic movement. 'I get the feeling you don't know your sister very well. She's as tough as blazes. She couldn't get hurt if you bounced her all the way to Paris.'

The comment took Laura's breath away. She struggled helplessly for adequate expression, glaring at him.

There was sexual mockery in the green eyes as he

watched her. 'If I were you, I'd mind my own business, Miss Laura Sloane. Your sister has a skin like a rhinoceros. I couldn't dent it if I tried.'

Before she could answer that, Annette herself had arrived beside them, giving Laura a stare which had daggers in it. 'Oh, you two have met,' she said without pleasure.

'You didn't tell me your sister was a beautiful blonde,' Simon Hilliard reproached her, his eyes switching to her with amusement.

Annette was not in the least amused. 'Let's dance,' she said, ignoring that remark and pulling at his arm possessively.

Donald had followed at her heels like a lost lamb, his shoulders hunched. He glared at the other man, blocking their way, aggression in the set of his jaw and the flush on his cheek.

Laura was afraid there was going to be some sort of scene. Donald looked like a man getting ready to pull the roof in on everyone. She sidestepped around Simon Hilliard and took hold of Donald's arm.

'I've got a headache, can we go now?' she asked plaintively, holding him back in case he tried to go for Simon Hilliard's throat.

Donald had a discontented, reluctant look, but his manners were too deeply entrenched for him to refuse to do as she asked. 'Of course,' he said sulkily, allowing her to lead him away. Just once he threw a look over his shoulder, but Laura did not halt, tugging at him to make him accompany her.

She persuaded him to let her drive. 'You don't want to get picked up for speeding, do you?' she asked. Donald sank into the passenger seat with a groan, shaking his head.

'You see what I meant about him,' he muttered.

'Oh, I saw.'

'What did you think of him?'

'I couldn't begin to tell you.'

Donald gave a heartfelt sigh. 'Annette's in love with him.'

'Nonsense,' Laura said vigorously.

He sat upright, a faintly hopeful expression in his eyes. 'You don't think she is?'

'Not in the slightest,' said Laura. Annette had too much in common with Simon Hilliard for that. He was right, damn him. Annette was thick-skinned and as tough as blazes. She was too involved with herself to be hurt by anyone else. She loved the image of herself which came back from mirrors and men's eyes. Annette was narcissistic, self-obsessed, self-willed. It was childish vanity which made her flirt with Simon Hilliard. She only truly existed in public when men were looking at her with admiration and desire—that made her feel real. And that, of course, was where Simon Hilliard could hurt her. If he started an affair with her and then walked away, Annette would see her mirror smashed, her image of herself as all-conquering and irresistible destroyed. It would not be an emotional wound, it would be a wound to the self-esteem.

'She seems very keen on him,' Donald protested.

'Oh, I've no doubt she finds him exciting,' Laura agreed. 'But that's a different matter.'

'I wish she found me exciting,' mourned Donald.

Laura looked at him with rueful understanding. She had had enough of Donald for one evening. In small doses he was rather sweet, but she had had a prolonged exposure to his company tonight, and she was no longer in a mood to listen to his defeated lack of self-confidence.

'I should have knocked his teeth down his throat,' he told her.

'Oh, that would have been a big help,' she sighed. One look at Simon Hilliard had told her that if Donald had started anything it would have been Donald flat on the floor within two seconds, and Annette was the sort of female who loves a winner. She would have looked at Donald's prone body with scorn before she twined herself all round Simon Hilliard in adoring delight. Of course, one couldn't tell Donald that. His ego was battered enough as it was.

'What has he got?' Donald asked of nobody in particular, staring out of the car with a moody face.

Laura decided not to answer that question. It might have taken her all night.

Shooting her a look, he accused: 'You said you didn't like him.'

'I know I did, and I meant it,' Laura assured him, turning the car into his street. 'I'll drop you and borrow your car until tomorrow. You can pick it up at my place, can't you?'

'Yes,' he said, his lower lip stuck out like a sulky baby. 'I believe you did like him.'

'I detested him,' said Laura as he got out of the car.

She said the same to her father next day. They had lunch together. It was the first time in months that she had seen him, and he was looking older, she thought. The strain of business was drawing lines in his smooth-fleshed face and giving his eyes a weary dullness.

'How's the firm?' she asked between courses, and he shrugged his wide shoulders.

'We're having a few problems. When aren't we? It

gets harder to chase business every year. About Annette—what are you doing to stop it? You can't just leave it at that. I told you the man was a swine. He was damned unscrupulous, the way he walked out on us—took some of our top electronic experts with him to start Siltel and promised them the earth if they'd go in with him.'

'Did he give them the earth?' Laura asked idly.

Her father played with the crumbs of his roll, his head bent. 'They stayed with him,' he admitted reluctantly.

'So maybe he did,' Laura deduced.

'He would have had to pay them to stay. Siltel keeps getting bigger. He has a great selling technique.'

'I know, I've seen it.'

George Sloane looked at her. 'What did you really make of him?'

'I detested him,' she said, as she had said to Donald.

'He's clever,' George Sloane said half-admiringly. 'And he has no ethics to get in his way. He has drive and energy and he knows what he's doing in the computer field.' He paused. 'I could kick myself for losing him,' he admitted.

That was quite an admission from her father and said a good deal for Simon Hilliard's rating as a business asset. Laura considered George Sloane as he talked about Annette. Her father was basically a very cold man, entirely centred on his business, driven by a need to succeed in the world. Laura had resented the way in which he had gradually shut her mother out of his life. He had rarely been at home and when he was he had treated Meriel Sloane with indifference. Laura had got the feeling that he forgot her when he wasn't in her company and she got the feeling that her mother knew it. George Sloane saw everyone and everything in terms of usefulness, and his wife had lost her usefulness to him very early on in their marriage.

It had been the company which had interested George Sloane in the beginning. Meriel Sloane had been an only child and George had wanted to take control of her father's firm. Once he had married her, though, he had lost interest in her except as the mother of his children. George Sloane had never been unfaithful, so far as Laura knew. He had been too cold-natured to chase other women. He had merely frozen Laura's mother to death. George Sloane was another man who despised women. Unlike Simon Hilliard he did not even have a sensual interest in them; he just didn't care for them at all.

His one passion was his business. That obsessed him. Looking at his tired face, she wondered if something was seriously wrong or if her father was just losing the energy which had made it possible for him to build up his firm.

'Even if I thought he'd marry her,' George Sloane said suddenly, 'I would want to stop it. Hilliard would love to get his greedy hands on my firm. He could run rings round Philip. Philip would be no match for him.' He picked up his wine glass and drained it, poured himself some more wine. 'Philip's no match for anyone,' he added, and Laura suddenly felt sorry for him. She saw that Philip was a disappointment to him. Philip did what he was told and George Sloane might once have thought that a quality he liked in his son but now he was beginning to realise that Philip's pliability was a flaw rather than an asset.

'Donald's the man I want for Annette. He'll make her a good husband. He's honest and straight.'

Not qualities Laura had somehow ever imagined she would hear her father praising. He had never been either, she suspected. His climb to power had been as unethical as Simon Hilliard's had been. She knew very little of the ins and outs of his business dealings, but she had watched him closely enough to know that her father was not above corkscrew tactics if he felt them necessary.

'Donald won't try to take the firm away from Philip; he'll support him.' George Sloane was talking almost without being aware who he was talking to and she wondered what was going through his mind. 'Hilliard is dangerous. He can see that I'm wide open. Philip's safe while I'm alive, but when I've gone it wouldn't be impossible for someone tough and unscrupulous to walk in there and grab the firm away from him.'

'But surely Philip would still have control as the major shareholder?'

'Hilliard could shunt him to one side without much difficulty,' her father admitted. 'If he talked the other shareholders round to his point of view, Philip would wind up just sitting there on the board, without a real voice in what went on.'

'You don't have much faith in Philip.'

He grimaced, arranging his cutlery in a pattern. 'Do you?'

Laura couldn't think of a thing to say. Her father looked up, giving a short laugh. 'No, exactly. But he's still my son, and I want him to run the business, not some jumped-up outsider with an eye to the main chance and no ethics to speak of.'

Laura wondered if, in his late middle age, her father was mellowing, or whether he had merely lost the drive which had carried him so far and was now ap-

preciating less forceful qualities. Now that he had got
to the top and knew he would be going no further, he
wanted to stay where he was and to make quite sure
that his son inherited what he had built. It was a pre-
dictable pattern. If her father feared Simon Hilliard, it
was because he feared the very qualities he recognised
as his own. He knew the possible danger of the other
man because he was viewing it from a knowledge of
how he himself would have acted in that position.

'I don't think you need to worry,' she pointed out. 'I
don't believe Simon Hilliard has any intention of
marrying Annette, even to get control of the firm.'

Her father did not look particularly comforted.
'Then what are his intentions?' he asked roughly.

Laura watched the waiter pour coffee into her cup.
She waited until the man had softly vanished again
before she said drily: 'I'll give you three guesses.'

'Damn him,' George Sloane muttered with his head
bent. 'What are we going to do about it?'

'I don't really see what we can do,' Laura told him,
her tone blunt. 'Annette is an adult—of sorts. Short of
having her kidnapped and locked up out of harm's way
I don't see what can be done.'

'She's in love with him, I suppose,' George Sloane
stated.

'Not on your life,' Laura retorted, as she had to
Donald.

Her father looked up. 'No?'

'She fancies him, that's all, but you know Annette.
You can't talk sense to her when she wants something.'

'And she wants Hilliard?'

Laura made a face. 'Oh, yes, and he's ready to give
her what she wants.'

A little red stole into her father's face. It amused Laura to see the angry embarrassment in his eyes. 'I don't find it funny,' he retorted, glaring at her.

'Neither do I,' Laura denied, shrugging. 'But I face facts. There's nothing we can do about it. I've talked to her. If you want any more than that done, you'll have to do it yourself.'

George Sloane slumped back in his chair. 'There must be some way of getting through to her what a mess she'll make of her life if she gets involved with Hilliard.'

Laura glanced at her watch. 'I'm afraid I must rush, Father—I have an appointment this afternoon. If you think of anything, let me know. You could always shoot Simon Hilliard, I suppose.' She rose and her father gave her an irascible look.

'I might just do that.'

CHAPTER THREE

On a fine summer morning the walk across the park was a pleasant experience, even carrying all the gear which she would need to use while she was working. She needed to get a first-hand glimpse of a heron. Photographs were never enough, but luckily London Zoo could always provide the living bird. Laura kept up a steady pace, filled with a sense of well-being, smiling at a gardener as she passed him clipping a hedge, the yellowy-green privet leaves shooting off in all directions, accompanied by that nostalgic smell of privet which is peculiarly associated with summer in the London suburbs.

Under a group of trees blue-black shadows shifted like spilled water, behind them the sunlight spreading in a dancing, glittering fall across the lake. Everywhere her eyes touched she felt a tingle of pleasure at what she saw. This early in the morning there were far fewer people around. Here and there someone was walking a dog or playing ball with a child, but otherwise the wide green spaces were empty and still glistening with overnight dew.

Laura's mood had no particular cause. She had awoken with a sense of happiness, an awareness of life which made everything she saw look new-washed and exciting.

On her way to the park she had darted across a road thick with traffic, almost under the wheels of a bus.

'Nearly got you!' the driver had yelled, laughing but wagging a reproving finger.

'Try again tomorrow,' Laura had invited, grinning back, because she had been so certain in her elated mood that nothing could touch her.

That was how she felt, she thought, as she went through the turnstile into the Zoo. She felt immortal this morning. She knew how the gods on Mount Olympus felt as they looked down over the sunlit world.

Before making her way to the aviary she made her ritual visit to the monkeys and stood for several minutes watching them swing and chatter on their bare branches, showing their teeth to each other. A couple of schoolboys gibbered back at them, leaping about. Laughing, Laura went off to find her heron, and discovered it in one of the Zoo ponds.

She did a series of drawings, trying to get the exact gradation of colour, the jointings of the fine thin legs. Now and then the heron would stalk about like Hamlet on the battlements of Elsinore, wrapped in brooding melancholy, and she would try to catch that blur of movement in a rapid sketch.

It was useful to someone writing children's books to be an artist, since children prefer their books to be illustrated. Laura had begun by writing a comic story with pictures and had moved on to doing factual books at her publisher's suggestion. It gave her the chance to do some ambitious illustrations, and the books sold well to schools and colleges.

She was just beginning to consider stopping when a party of Japanese visitors swarmed down the path, cameras clicking. Laura glanced at them in vague interest, then did a double-take as she recognised Simon Hilliard in the middle of them, a tiny, doll-like Japanese child attached to each hand, their feet scampering like the paws of mice to keep up with his long strides, although he was trying to suit his steps to theirs without quite managing it. He was talking too, bending towards them, first one and then the other, his face full of that teasing look which she had seen on it so many times now that she began to think it was his usual expression. She was staggered to realise that he was talking in their language and that apparently they understood every word, judging by the giggles with which they greeted what he said.

He straightened, still laughing, and saw Laura. His eyes were already moving away from her when they performed a rapid slant back again, and she realised that for the first second he hadn't recognised her.

He detached himself from the party and came towards her, his little companions still clutching his hands. They were between five and seven, Laura guessed, not the same age but close together in years and sisters, she suspected. Their bobbed black hair, round black eyes and cherry pink lips somehow gave them a sort of beauty which was yet consistent with childhood; cute, she thought, looking down at them, or should it be adorable?

'What are you doing here?' Simon's eyes shifted from her face to her easel.

'Working.'

'Working?' He moved round and scrutinised the heron sketches on the easel. 'Are you an artist?'

Laura didn't quite like the surprise in the tone. 'I illustrate children's books.' She was faintly defensive, half expecting him to laugh. Sometimes people did, when she told them. Quite a lot of people couldn't take her job seriously as a way of earning a living. They

thought she just played at it, especially if they knew
how wealthy her father was. They imagined she must
do her books just to pass the time, keep herself
amused.

Simon Hilliard didn't laugh. He studied her without
expression. 'Do they get published?'

She was half inclined to quarrel with the question,
sensing a hidden mockery behind it, but she decided
to answer it straight. 'Yes.' She paused, then added
with tart self-congratulation, 'And they sell.'

'Well done,' he returned in smooth, grave tones, a
suspicion of a smile touching his mouth. He slid his
eyes down her white cotton jeans and then up again
over the blue cotton top which her small, high breasts
strained against as she adjusted the clip holding the
paper on the easel. Laura felt a faint flush at his scru-
tiny, aware of it although she had looked away from
him. The last thing she wanted was to be aware of
Simon Hilliard in any way whatever, and she wished
he would stop looking at her in that way.

One of the little girls tugged at his hand. He glanced
down, a ready smile appearing, and she said something
in her own tongue, pointing at Laura's sketches.

'Kiri says she likes that,' Simon told Laura, looking
at her again. 'They have funny birds like that in Japan,
she says.'

Laura flipped the used sheet over the top of the
easel and smiled at the little girl. 'If she'll stand still,
I'll do a souvenir portrait for her,' she offered.

Simon relayed this and the child beamed from ear to
ear, her open vanity and self-confidence making
the two adults look at each other with suppressed
smiles. Kiri stood very still, staring with those round
dark eyes, while Laura worked, giving quick glances at

her and then glancing at the heron.

When she detached the sheet and offered it to her, Kiri and her sister began to laugh as they saw what Laura had done. Simon looked over their bent heads, his face also breaking into laughter.

Kiri was shown trotting along with the heron, long and lanky and ungainly in a very grand fashion, the child attached to him by his grey wing feathers.

'Why do I get the feeling that that's meant to be me?' Simon asked softly.

Laura didn't answer. She was doing a second sketch for the other little girl. This time she drew her riding on the heron's back, his long thin legs in hurried motion. As an afterthought she added a definite jockey's cap to the little girl's bobbed head.

Chattering, the little girls compared drawings, then thanked Laura again with curtseys and smiles which more than made up for their lack of English.

'Very kind of you,' Simon drawled as his charges sat down on the grass nearby, their attention entirely given over to contemplation of their own beauty as shown in Laura's drawings.

'I like children.' Staring at the little girls, she added: 'When I was five I had a Japanese doll. She had a red satin kimono and a big yellow sash. I must find her when I get home.' Catching his surprised look, she shrugged in self-derision. 'I'm afraid I never throw anything away. I'm a great hoarder.'

'Unconsidered trifles in every box?'

'Something like that. It's a great mistake. You can get bogged down in *things*.'

'Fatál,' he agreed. 'Now, I'm the opposite. I abandon everything as soon as I can. I'm not struggling through life weighed down with things I don't need.'

'Like a wife,' Laura suggested before she had realised what she was going to say and at once regretting having said it.

'Like a wife,' he drawled, meeting her eyes. The slight truce which they had set up over the innocent heads of the children dissolved. She had been stupid to let that remark slip. It had made the sexual barrier come up again.

Hurriedly she asked: 'What are you doing with them, anyway?'

'Their father's a friend of mine. He's in London on a selling expedition. His wife has gone shopping in Oxford Street this morning, so I offered to help him babysit.'

It didn't quite chime with what she knew of him. She had not seen him as a man who loved children. She would have expected him to regard them as tiresome appendages, domestic responsibilities which he preferred to do without.

He was wearing a suit this morning, the lightweight material tailored to emphasise his height and lithe build, the pale blue of it set off by a darker shirt. Laura wondered why he chose to wear a very expensive suit to the Zoo and decided it was to impress the Japanese businessman who was his friend.

Was that why he had offered to play nursemaid to the children, too? Her wandering glance rose from examination of his clothes to his face and found him watching her with lifted brows.

'How do I rate?'

Solemnly, Laura said: 'Passable.'

'You're very kind.' Mockery sparkled in the green eyes. 'I must say, you look very fetching in that workmanlike gear. The odd thing about jeans is that they look so sexy on a girl, especially when they're a size too small.'

Laura involuntarily looked down at her own jeans. 'Mine aren't . . .' she began, and then stopped, giving him a crisp smile. 'Witty, aren't you?'

He grinned at her. The little girls were spilling out an excited flood of words to a smiling man in a grey suit who had stolled up. He admired their drawings before turning towards Laura and Simon. 'Yashi,' said Simon, 'may I introduce Laura Sloane? Laura, this is Yashi Loshoto.'

Yashi bowed with smiling formality before taking her hand. His hair was as black as his daughters', his face thin and intelligent.

'Very kind of you to do the pictures for my daughters,' he thanked her in beautiful English. 'They are very pleased with them. They will make very happy souvenirs of their visit.'

'I'm glad they like them,' Laura said.

He looked at her easel. 'You are an artist?'

Laura explained again and he listened with interested gravity, watching her face as though trying to dig beneath the cultural barrier which their different races set up between them, his dark eyes humanely sympathetic.

'You write the stories as well?' Simon asked, and Laura looked at him, the smooth blonde flick of her hair revealing the pale delicacy of her cheek, sunlight picking out the tiny golden hairs which gave her skin a downy softness.

'Yes, I do both pictures and text.'

'Talented,' he commented.

His friend asked politely: 'You have finished work for today?'

'I think so,' Laura nodded. 'I've done what I came here to do.'

He gave one of his polite little bows. 'Will you permit me to give you lunch? The children would be delighted.' He spoke to them and they gave that excited trill in answer, their round dark eyes delighted as they looked at Laura.

Their father gestured, smiling. 'You see? They hope you will come with us.'

She hesitated, knowing that if Simon Hilliard had not been with them she might well have agreed since it fascinated her to watch the little girls' facial expressions, see those dark eyes dancing with lively enjoyment.

'That's very kind,' she began, meaning to refuse, and Simon himself interrupted, his hand closing around her arm and silencing her.

'She'd love to—why don't you walk on with the girls, Yashi? I'll come along with Laura when we've packed up her stuff.'

The other nodded, smiling, and led his daughters away, his head bent to listen to their talk. They skipped beside him, trying to keep up with his faster steps.

Laura looked up at Simon, her face impatient. 'Why did you say that? I didn't intend to come.'

'So I saw, but that was why I accepted for you. Yashi has old-fashioned ideas about gratitude. He could have been hurt if you'd refused his hospitality after you'd done his children a favour like that. He would have gone home grieving at the thought that he hadn't returned your kindness and it would have nagged away at him for years.'

She laughed at the teasing in his face but said: 'Don't be absurd!

Still smiling, he said: 'I'm serious. You don't know him. He worships those kids, and any kindness done to them is done to him.'

Laura thought about that. 'That's rather nice.'

'Very nice,' Simon agreed. 'Yashi is quite a guy. The more I know him the more I admire and respect him.'

'How do you come to speak Japanese, anyway?' Laura asked, beginning to pack up her things.

He helped without thought, folding her stool and collecting up a pile of charcoal and pencil stubs. 'I've a flair for languages. I pick them up almost without trying. It's just a knack.'

'A very useful one. I've no talent in that direction.'

'You have plenty of talent in other directions,' he said, and he might have been referring to her drawing, if it had not been for the sexual mockery in the green eyes which made it clear he meant nothing of the kind.

Laura said crisply: 'Don't waste your time flirting with me!'

The green eyes sharpened. 'Does it work?'

She regarded him warily. 'What?'

'The Snow Queen stuff,' he mocked. 'Does your hands-off sign keep the men away? Or is it intended to do just the opposite, I wonder?'

Laura found the intimate inspection of his gaze disturbing. He was the sort of man who refused to allow consciousness of the sexual gulf to fade from the mind. She had to fight a desire to back away physically, as well as mentally, from the constant, confusing shift of the green eyes as they made an apparently itemised tour of every inch of her.

She stiffened her back, holding her portfolio like a

weapon. 'You'll just have to make up your own mind about that, won't you?'

'You have a habit of doing that,' he complained.

'You have a habit of making irrelevant remarks,' Laura muttered, wishing she dared hit him with the portfolio.

She got the feeling he knew what was in her mind. He grinned. 'If you're going to do it, do it,' he invited.

She evaded that. 'What do I have the habit of doing?'

'Throwing out challenges and then backing off,' he drawled.

'I think you misunderstood me,' Laura informed him with icy withdrawal.

'I don't think so.'

'Deliberately,' she added, giving him a direct and angry look.

'Coward,' he taunted, laughing under his breath at that expression on her face. 'Made up your mind whether or not to accept that bet?'

'The very suggestion is despicable.'

'Ah, but I'm a realist,' he told her, a dry note entering his voice. 'You seem to know nothing of your own sex, or to pretend not to. Women are like cats—a wise man may play with them, but he doesn't try to own one. Give a woman the idea that she has you on a lead, and she starts to give you hell. Women despise men who show them any weak spots. Like cats, they're fond of using their claws and they enjoy hurting for its own sake.'

Laura was silenced by the drily delivered attack. 'You really don't like us, do you?' she said at last, unable to hide the fact that he had shaken her.

The look he bent on her had charm in it now and

she sensed that he was half irritated with himself for having said as much as he had. Now he was hurriedly covering up, retreating fast.

'On the contrary, I like you very much. I've got a passion for pretty things.'

'Chauvinist,' Laura said absently, wondering if he realised that that remark had been as sexually contemptuous as the long dry speech which had preceded it.

'We'd better catch up to Yashi, he must be wondering where we've got to,' said Simon, moving away.

Laura recognised a certain truth in what he had said about women, at least as far as it applied to Annette. Her sister despised poor harmless Donald because she could do what she liked with him. There was that much of the cat in her that she could be ruthless in using her claws if she could get away with it, but when she came up against someone stronger and tougher she would twine herself silkily around them, purring invitingly. Annette had sense enough to realise that Simon Hilliard was too tough for her to try using her claws; Laura had seen that much while she watched them together at the party. Annette was in the weaker position for once and she knew it. That was what made Simon Hilliard so dangerous.

His view of women revealed a self-involved sexual attitude which bothered Laura. He had made no attempt to hide his opinion of her sex, although she suspected that after his little outburst he had regretted saying so much to her. She resented his attitude, both on her own behalf and on behalf of her whole sex. No one had the right to make such generalisations about other human beings. The hard, cynical green eyes had underlined his feelings as she looked into them.

The Zoo was crowded with parties of school-children, eating packets of sandwiches and bananas on benches, their flushed and tired faces excited as they talked to each other. Laura and Simon found Yashi and his little girls near the canal, watching a boat full of tourists passing on the way to Camden Town. The little girls were waving, dancing up and down on the spot, and some people on the boat waved back.

'Ah, there you are,' said Yashi, giving them an apparently solemn look which hid, nevertheless, a quiet amusement. 'We began to wonder if you had eloped.'

'It crossed my mind,' said Simon, grinning.

'It didn't cross mine,' Laura informed them, and Yashi's dark eyes sidled to her, open laughter in them. Simon laughed, too, but that glow had come into the green eyes again. He didn't like the implication of her remark. His vanity had been hurt, she thought. He was a man whose sense of humour did not extend to his own powers of sexual attraction. Like Annette, he preferred to see himself as all-conquering and irresistible, no doubt, especially in front of another man.

Yashi and his little girls walked on and Simon fell into step beside Laura, giving her a hard stare. 'Was that intended to make me lose face?'

'Mirror, mirror,' Laura murmured.

'What?' He asked, frowning.

She didn't bother to explain. 'Losing face is an Oriental concept.'

'We may not have given it the same importance in the West, but we have it, all the same,' Simon said through his teeth. 'I think you know that. I think you knew it when you said that to Yashi.'

'Rise above it,' Laura advised softly.

'Patronise me, madam, and you'll regret it,' he told

her with a crisp intonation. 'Resist the temptation to put me down in front of Yashi—he sees the battle of the sexes in the light of his own culture and he would think a lot less of me if I let a woman get the better of me.'

Laura shrugged. 'If we're talking about resisting temptation, may I suggest you try doing it yourself? Make any sexist remarks about or to me and you'll get what you're asking for!'

He halted mid-stride, turning a frowning dark face towards her. There was a little silence, then he said: 'That was quite a speech.'

'I meant it,' Laura assured him, walking on.

He caught up with her. 'Was that your answer to what I said earlier about women?'

'It was my warning about what would happen if you tried to give Yashi the wrong impression about me,' Laura told him calmly. 'Losing face isn't confined to one sex.'

He thought that over. 'You're a chip off the old block,' he told her at last. 'My first impression of you was right. You're your father's daughter.'

'I can't dispute that.'

'Would you like to?' He shot her an interrogative glance. Laura felt it, but her face stayed blank.

'If you're asking what I think of my father, don't bother. I wouldn't tell you under any circumstances.'

'Why not?'

'It's none of your business, and I'm not unaware that you don't like him.'

He laughed shortly. 'You phrase that very cautiously. Try again. I hate his guts.'

'Why?' Laura asked, staring ahead. She wondered if he would tell her and waited for his answer with a strong sense of curiosity.

'That's a long story,' he said, and she knew he wasn't going to tell her. His voice had withdrawn. When she looked at him he was smiling and behind the handsome mask of that face she sensed a cold, deliberate rage. Whatever the reason for the animosity between Simon Hilliard and her father, it went deep, and the way her father ran his business had nothing to do with it, she was convinced.

'Is that why you're chasing Annette?'

He gave her a mocking look. 'I thought it was the other way round.'

'You're so modest, Mr Hilliard,' Laura said bitingly.

'She is a woman and therefore to be won,' he quoted. Laura vaguely recognised the quotation but couldn't place it. She could, however, place the sexual over-confidence.

'I'm beginning to hope Annette turns you down flat,' she snapped. 'I'd like to see you get your come-uppance.'

'I shall be sorry to disappoint you,' he taunted.

'Don't count your chickens.'

'Some chicken,' he murmured, grinning. 'Your sister is a very sexy creature.'

'If she could hear the way you talk about her, she'd run like blazes.'

'She'd be flattered,' he assured her. 'That's how she sees herself.'

Was it? Laura wondered. Probably, yes, and it was maddening that he should see Annette so clearly. It would make it much easier if he could be proved wrong about her, but Laura had a sinking feeling that he would be proved absolutely right. Annette never had been able to resist snatching something she wanted, and the fact that this man was mockingly evading her would make him all the more desirable. That, of course, was the technique he was employing, knowing what he was doing. He had summed Annette up far too accurately and was leading her away like the Pied Piper, keeping one step ahead and always just out of reach, knowing that Annette would run after him, desperate to prove to herself that she could capture him.

The trouble with Annette was that she believed her own publicity. She revelled in the legend of her power over the opposite sex, and no one was going to smash Annette's legend if she could help it.

They had lunch on a boat on the Regent's Canal. The little girls were reluctant with their food, disliking the alien look and smell of it, but their father persisted, eager to have them broaden their outlook.

'Children always dislike strange foods, don't they?' Laura told him as Kiri picked at her meal. 'I expect she would love beefburgers, though.'

Kiri looked up, black eyes sparkling. 'Beefburgers,' she said distinctly, and they all laughed.

'Coke,' Kiri added, delighted with this success.

'You're beginning to speak English very well,' Laura told her, and Yashi translated, smiling. Kiri gave Laura a demure look, her mouth curving, extremely pleased with herself.

The other little girl sighed deeply, and Yashi gave her an indulgent glance. 'She wants to leave her lunch,' he explained. 'But she must try to like it. We must all try to learn, mustn't we?' He translated that for his little girl, who made a face but went on valiantly trying to like the food which did not taste half as good to her as her own home cooking.

'Do you like English food, Yashi?' Laura asked.

His quiet look had humour in it. 'I like bacon and egg,' he admitted. 'English breakfast—very good.'

'I've never eaten Japanese food, so you're one up on me,' Laura told him.

'One up?' He repeated, puzzled.

'You have an advantage,' Laura explained.

His face broke into a broad smile. 'I see. Then you must try some Japanese food.' He looked sideways at Simon. 'Perhaps one evening you will bring Laura to have dinner with us? My wife would be charmed to meet her. She has not yet met many English ladies, and she was hoping she would do so while she was here.'

Simon regarded Laura, one dark brow curving mockingly. 'I'm sure Laura would love to meet your wife.'

Faced with them both Laura had no option but to say warmly: 'I'd love to.'

Simon's mouth twitched in bland appreciation of her position. 'I knew you would,' he said.

Laura longed to hit him, but she suppressed the desire, smiling very sweetly at him as though butter wouldn't melt in her mouth.

When they left the restaurant the towpath running beside it was bathed in a golden sunshine which made the canal water glint and dance and threw a brilliant net over the park, making the stretching green lawns glitter and the oak and sycamore trees throw wide pools of black shadow.

'I've enjoyed meeting you very much,' Laura said as she thanked Yashi for the lunch. 'I hope you enjoy the rest of your stay in England.'

'But we will meet again,' he assured her, giving that

formal little bow. 'You have promised. You must let my wife and myself teach you to like Japanese food.'

Simon watched, eyes glinting. 'I'll bring her,' he told Yashi. 'We must fix it up soon.'

Laura turned away to smile at the little girls. They gave her their hands and curtsied in little bobs, the extreme courtesy of their manner making her smile again, but delighting her.

'I'll put you in a taxi,' Simon offered.

'I'll walk back.'

'Not with all that stuff.' He looked at the folded stool, the easel and her various boxes of charcoal, pencil and paint.

'I'm used to it. I always walk across the park.'

'Well, this time you'll take a taxi.'

Laura began to argue and caught the hardness in his eyes. She closed her mouth. He steered her towards the road and muttered drily: 'Thank you. Yashi expects an English lady to have better manners.'

'I'm sorry to disappoint Yashi, of course, but I run my life my own way, and that includes walking when I prefer to, rather than take a totally unnecessary taxi.'

'Unnecessary or not, I'd offered to get you one and if you'd refused I'd have lost face.'

She gave him a wry look. 'You seem to set more store by losing face than Yashi does.'

'I know him. You don't. He was horrified at the idea of you lugging all that gear across the park in sweltering sunshine.'

'I'm not made of sugar. I won't melt.'

'Yashi believes all women are made of sugar.'

'It's time he looked around and realised they're not, then.'

Simon breathed out a long, angry sigh. 'You're beginning to annoy me.'

He was looking away from her, signalling to a passing taxi. It darted through the stream of traffic and pulled to a halt beside them, engine running. Simon loaded her gear into it. 'Address?' he asked casually and Laura gave it without thinking before something about the green gleam of his eyes made her look at him suspiciously.

He repeated the address to the driver and the taxi began to pull away. Laura chewed impatiently on her lower lip. There was a warning prickle running down her spine. She hadn't liked the way Simon Hilliard smiled at her as the taxi began to move away from him.

CHAPTER FOUR

LAURA worked with a half-distracted mind that afternoon. The light was fast approaching a soft dusk and she would have to stop soon, but she was determined to get some work done. She did not want to think about the subject to which her mind kept straying. It had given her a shock to realise in what direction it was straying, at first. Simon Hilliard had no business inside her head. She angrily pushed him out, but he came drifting back a moment later. That man needs to be taken down a peg or two, she thought, teeth set.

When the doorbell went she flung down her paintbrush with a muttered exclamation. Who was this? Was there no peace?

When she opened the door and found Annette leaning against the frame in one of her graceful attitudes, her bright head propped by one beautifully manicured hand, Laura looked at her without surprise but with unhidden displeasure. 'Now what?'

'I've got a few things to say to you,' Annette informed her, pushing past without an invitation. Laura closed the door and followed her, summoning up the energy to counter whatever was coming.

'What do you think you're up to?' Annette demanded, swinging round on her, hands on her hips. 'What was all that about with Donald at my party? Are you after him?'

To give herself time to think, Laura passed a hand

over her hair, smoothing it down. 'Want some tea?'

'I asked you a question!'

'It was a damned silly question.'

'Just answer it,' Annette commanded, giving her a stare of sisterly dislike which Laura returned with interest.

'You don't want Donald, so what's it to do with you what he does or with whom?'

'I thought so!' Annette showed all her little white teeth in a feline sneer. 'You're chasing him!'

'If I was, I'd have caught him by now,' Laura shrugged. 'It isn't hard or he wouldn't have fallen for you.'

Annette drew an impeded breath. 'Is that so? I see, that's how it is, is it!' Her face reflected rapid and infuriated thinking. Annette wasn't much used to such occupation. She couldn't think and talk at the same time. Laura had often noticed it. Annette said whatever came into her head while she was trying to work out what had been said to her and decide how to deal with it.

Having caught her off balance, Laura decided to finish the job. 'Going to Paris?' she asked casually, moving off towards the kitchen as she spoke.

'What if I am?' Annette squeaked, pursuing her, hot on her heels.

'Just curious.'

'You want to know so that you can tell Donald!'

'No, I just wondered if I'd win my bet.'

'What bet?'

Laura filled the kettle and plugged it into the socket, then reached up to get some cups out. Annette hovered behind her, trying to watch her face and not succeeding very well.

'What bet?' she repeated through her clenched teeth.

'The one I've got with Simon Hilliard.'

'What?' Annette's voice swooped in fury.

'If you want some tea would you mind passing me the milk from the fridge?' Laura asked politely.

'I don't believe you,' snapped Annette, hot colour rushing up her face. 'You're lying. I know the way your mind works. You're just trying to put me off him.'

'Why should I? You can't have it both ways. If you really think I'm chasing Donald you can't believe I'd try to stop you going to Paris with another man.'

Annette thought that over, chewing on her lower lip, her lovely face childish.

'Milk, please,' Laura reminded, and her sister absentmindedly got the bottle out of the fridge and passed it to her. Laura poured out tea while Annette continued to ruminate.

'Simon bet you he'd take me to Paris?'

'Sure of himself, isn't he?' Laura gave her a cheerful smile. 'He really thinks he has you tied up in pink ribbons.'

'Oh!' snapped Annette, grinding her teeth. 'Oh, does he? The beast! And he made a bet with you . . . Oh, I could scream!'

'Not here,' Laura begged. 'The neighbours wouldn't like it. Have some tea.'

Annette accepted a cup without noticing. 'He actually bet you that I'd go to Paris with him?' Her face was beetroot red now and she seemed to be having difficulty with her breathing.

'He was so sure he was on to a good thing,' Laura murmured.

'Oh, was he?' Annette with a wild gesture flung her cup, tea splashing everywhere, into the sink. There was a crash and splintering of china, then she swung on her heel and rushed out of the kitchen. Laura heard her slam out of the front door. She looked at the broken cup, the splashes of tea staining the tiled wall, the draining board, and biting her lip, she tried not to laugh. It wasn't really funny. Poor Annette! She hadn't even had to lie to her, just tell her the absolute truth.

And although Annette had been so furious, Laura suspected she had heard a note almost of relief behind her sister's voice. That vein of common sense again, she decided. Donald was so much more obviously a marrying man, and Annette wasn't the type to leap into the dark. She was rather attracted by the idea of a secure and cosseted future. She might have been tempted by Simon Hilliard's dark good looks and charm, but half of her had been dragging its feet, reminding her that he was very unlikely to offer her any future, except of a limited duration and of a very definite sort.

Laura tidied up, reflecting that the loss of one cup was a small price to pay for having put a stop to Simon Hilliard, and then went back to work, her mind now entirely in control of itself, absorbed once more into the business of transferring her own view of the world on to paper.

Her publisher rang next morning, his voice cheerful. 'Just checking on the progress of the new book. Going well?'

'Stop worrying, Declan. It's going at the usual pace.'

'Think you'll meet the deadline?'

'If people don't ring me up too often.'

'Sorry,' he said, laughing. 'Look, would it hold you up too much to have lunch? We haven't seen anything of each other lately. I've got nothing down for next Wednesday.'

'And you want me to fill the hole in your lunch date book?' Laura was laughing, too, because Declan Neale had that effect on her. He was the junior partner, a broad-shouldered, pugnacious Celt with lively hazel eyes and a strong sense of humour. From time to time they saw each other in a social way, although their relationship had never progressed beyond a companionable friendship. Declan lived at great speed, talking twice as fast as anyone Laura had ever met, spawning ideas at a speed almost as fast, and never lacking the courage to put them into operation. If one of his ideas flopped, Declan shrugged and turned to another, forgetting all about the momentary failure.

'I want to have a pleasant cosy chat,' he said. 'I've had a little idea.'

'That sounds ominous,' Laura commented, recalling some of his past ideas without enthusiasm.

'We could talk it over,' he suggested. 'Next Wednesday?'

'Fine,' said Laura, knowing that he would keep pressing until she agreed. Declan in pursuit of one of his little ideas was unstoppable.

'That's marvellous,' he said, the lingering trace of a Welsh childhood overlaying his London accent. He was the only partner in the firm whom Laura had ever met. The senior partner lived in a remote office into which she had never penetrated. It was rumoured that he sometimes emerged to touch hands with best-selling authors with royal condescension before scuttling back to his eyrie again, leaving Declan to deal with all other more mundane matters. Declan's father had run the firm until his death. Laura was not sure exactly what the senior partner did, or even whether he did anything, apart from balance the books and drink good sherry.

When he had rung off she returned to work, forgetting all about him. Laura had an odd, stubborn individual mind with a drive towards independence which she had never consciously rationalised. From an early age she had learnt to stand on her own two feet, both emotionally and intellectually, and it was this difficult, strong-grained personality which always so surprised the men who were attracted to her delicate blonde looks. They could not match the two. Men who found that visual femininity so appealing did not find her habit of independence at all admirable.

They always wanted her to lean and yield, letting them take her over as though she were some twining bindweed only looking for something strong to attach itself to. Laura, however, demanded to be treated as a person, refusing to give herself up to the possession of someone who saw only her exterior and did not wish to know anything of what lay beneath the surface. In her experience, men tended to try to grab at too early a stage. They never gave a relationship time to grow. Denied, they were apt to become sulky, accusing, like little boys cheated of a toy they had their hearts set on.

I must attract the wrong men, she had often thought. Is that really all they want? Knowing nothing of her but her smooth skin, blonde hair and big blue eyes, they were apparently desperate to get her into bed and angry if she refused. Was it some sort of tribal test of manhood? Did they feel impelled to demand submission from every female they met merely to prove themselves male? Or was it something in Laura herself which made them imagine she would fall into their arms on a first date and be meltingly persuadable?

If she tried to ask them questions like that, though, it either made them furious, or brought on a further attempt to persuade her with the implication that it was Laura who was being tested, her femininity under inspection. If she still refused they would accuse her of being frigid. 'I can alter that,' one of them once said.

'Thank you, but I like the way I am,' Laura had replied gravely, and had seen his face turn sulky.

'What are you waiting for? Not a wedding ring?' He had given a sneer and Laura had looked at him without favour.

'I'm very expensive. At the very least a diamond bracelet,' she had mocked, her open amusement infuriating him.

She wasn't in fact sure what it was she was waiting for—perhaps an untapped reservoir inside herself, a flare of real sexual attraction which she had never felt. Whatever it was, it had never happened yet. Sometimes she wondered if it ever would.

She broke off at one to snatch a quick salad lunch and was back at work within the hour, her attention completely given to her work. When the doorbell went during the afternoon she straightened, her back aching and a crick in her neck. Annette again? She went to open the door wondering what new crisis had arisen, but when she looked into Simon Hilliard's face her tiredness fell away and she felt a sting of excitement coupled with her immediate defensive wariness.

'Oh. Hello.'

His brows swooped up at her tone. 'That's what I like, a warm welcome everywhere I go.'

She barred his entry, holding the door as though about to slam it in his face. 'What do you want?'

'We have a date to fix.'

'A date?' She stared, stiffening.

His green eyes mocked. 'With Yashi, remember?'

Laura remembered, her lips tightening. 'It was very kind of him to invite me, but . . .'

'No buts. He would be very offended if I didn't produce you. His wife was delighted with the drawings of their little girls.'

'I'm glad,' Laura returned. 'But I'm very busy.'

'Busy doing what?'

'Working.'

'In the evenings?' He was making fun of her and the amusement in the catlike eyes kindled an answering amusement in Laura, but she refused to let him see it.

'I work all the hours God sends. I have this very demanding publisher.'

'Change your publisher,' he recommended. His hand slid down the door and suddenly Laura found herself moved out of the way while Simon Hilliard inserted himself deftly into the flat and closed the door behind him.

'Now look——' she began, and he put a finger on her lips, shaking his black head at her.

'Nasty! You're a very difficult girl.' He sauntered away and stood eyeing her work, his hands in his pockets, his long body at ease in a casual fashion which made it clear he had no intention of budging. 'You're very clever,' he told her.

'How kind!'

Her sarcasm made him laugh, his eyes shooting

sideways at her. 'What have you been up to with Annette?' he asked with a sudden challenge which left her
too off balance to know what to say.

'What?' She temporized, hoping to think of some
answer in a moment.

'She had a date with me last night, but she stood me
up.'

'Oh, did she?' Laura's mouth curled up at the edges
while he watched her with dry observation.

'Like that, do you? I thought you might. And I've
got a shrewd idea it was your hand that chucked a
spanner in the works.'

'I'm sure you'll find consolation,' Laura shrugged,
abandoning any pretence of not knowing what he was
talking about.

'Oh, I intend to,' he said smoothly in a way she did
not much like. 'But just for the record, how did you do
it? I like to know these little things for future refer-
ence.'

'Maybe Annette just got bored with you?' Laura
suggested, tongue in cheek. 'It could happen.' She
paused, smiling. 'Even with someone as fascinating as
yourself.'

'You little bitch,' he said, his smile breaking into
laughter. 'But we both know it didn't happen like that,
don't we?'

'Oh, of course,' Laura agreed sweetly. 'Unthinkable,
isn't it? That any girl could get bored with you?'

He flicked a long finger down her cheek and she had
to fight a temptation to leap away, so strangely did
that brief touch affect her. Her skin seemed to carry
the trace of his touch like the searing of fire for
minutes afterwards.

'I could get annoyed with you,' he murmured, still smiling. 'At a guess, I'd say you dripped some sort of poison into her ear. I barely know you, but instinct warns me that you have the Borgia touch.'

'You'd better be careful, then, hadn't you?' Laura glanced at her watch very obviously. 'I'm rather busy, Mr Hilliard. If you don't mind . . .' She moved away towards the door.

'Tomorrow night?' he asked, without moving, his hands in his pockets and his black head tilted towards her with an enquiring look.

'I liked Yashi,' said Laura, sighing. 'And I'm sure his wife is charming, but . . .'

'You have a passion for that word. No buts. Tomorrow night?'

Laura met the quizzical green eyes with impatience. 'Don't try to bulldoze me, Mr Hilliard.'

'I'll pick you up at seven.' He smiled at her. 'And leave your armour off tomorrow night. Remember Yashi has fixed ideas about women and he admires your beautiful blonde looks. He wouldn't much appreciate watching you carve me up over the dinner table.'

He had gone before she had thought of an answer to that. It was only as she was trying to bend her reluctant mind to work again that it occurred to her that for the first time she had met a man who apparently saw through her outer appearance to the mind behind it without being surprised or alarmed.

She wasn't surprised to hear that Annette had stood him up the night before, but she couldn't help wondering how long Annette's fury with him would last. It depended, she imagined, on how strong her sister's feelings towards him were, and whether he would be able to talk Annette round. Once he discovered what Laura had said he might lie his way out of it. She paused to look up at the window, watching a threatening black cloud which was hanging overhead with dark intentions of raining on them at any minute. Or would he lie? She considered his character thoughtfully. No, she decided, Simon Hilliard wouldn't bother. He would no doubt laugh and admit everything, say teasingly that it was a joke. And would Annette fall for that? Yes, she might well. She was daft enough to shrug the whole thing off while her infatuation for him lasted.

The cloud disgorged its burden and rain began to stream down the windows with a rushing sound. Laura abandoned her attempt to concentrate. Her mind had been too disturbed by Simon Hilliard's visit. She went into the kitchen to make herself some coffee instead.

She was tempted to ring Annette to find out how things were shaping, but decided it was wisest to leave well enough alone. That evening she sat watching a long documentary about Japan which providentially had appeared on the screen. It would be useful to know something about Yashi's home land the following evening. Towards the end of it the phone rang. Laura turned down the set and answered it warily. At this hour of the night it might be a heavy breather. It was, in a sense, since it was Donald, apparently in a state of extreme excitement.

'She said yes!' he gabbled.

'Yes?' Laura adjusted her thoughts and caught on. 'She did? When?'

'Just now. We're having a celebratory drink. To-morrow we're going to buy the ring.'

'Congratulations, Donald. Give her my love.'

'I can't believe it!' She got the impression Donald had had several celebratory drinks already, or maybe he had given himself some Dutch courage before pro-posing. His voice had a thickened, slurred sound. 'I just can't believe my luck!'

Love had scored another of his ironic hits, Laura decided. Donald might not congratulate himself on his luck in a few years' time, but then on the other hand, he might be rapturously happy for life. 'I'm very pleased you're so happy,' she compromised.

'I thought a diamond,' Donald went on. 'Don't you?'

He was in the stage of being drunk when his conver-sation moved at a tangent. Laura had to think for a few seconds before she realised what he meant. 'The ring? I should let Annette decide that.' Annette would, anyway, whether Donald knew it or not. 'She'd prob-ably like a diamond, though.' Or a sapphire, or a ruby, or anything large and sufficiently impressive.

'Hilliard never meant a thing to her, you know,' Donald assured her with a hint of aggression. 'Not a thing. She says so.'

'Good,' said Laura, eyebrows raised. Did he believe that? Did he expect her to believe it?

'I knew you'd be pleased,' he said. 'I wanted you to be the first to know. I'd ring my mother, but at this time of night ...' His voice trailed off. Laura could imagine what his mother would say, at this or any time of night. Annette wasn't exactly every mother's idea of a blushing bride. 'I wanted to tell someone,' Donald added, pathetically.

'I'm glad you thought of me, then,' Laura promised, feeling very sorry for him. What was Annette doing? Drinking champagne, no doubt, and planning the size and price of her engagement ring.

'My future sister-in-law,' he said, growing maudlin. 'I've never had one before.'

'Well, you'll have one now,' said Laura, wondering how much longer he was going to keep her standing here talking.

'That's nice,' he said. 'I like you, Laura. You've been very good to me. I wanted to tell you first.'

'Well, goodnight, Donald, thank you,' she said hopefully.

He did take the hint at last and rang off. Laura switched off the silent TV and sat down to think. Annette hadn't wasted any time. It was quite flattering, really. Her sister had been suspicious of her own motives, Laura recognised, and had proceeded to nail Donald without delay before Laura could get to work on him. Poor Donald, he hadn't had a chance. But then he wouldn't see it like that. He was believing himself at this moment to be the happiest man in the world—and maybe he was, if it was true that ignorance was bliss. I hope Annette is going to be good to him, thought Laura. Donald made her feel like a puppy in a pet shop window with the notice: good home wanted for stray, pinned above him.

She went to bed some time later and slept through her alarm clock, a very rare occurrence. When she did open her eyes she felt oddly heavy and lethargic despite her long, deep sleep. Reluctantly slipping out of bed, she felt a pain shoot across her temples. Her throat was raw and dry and as she huddled into her dressing-gown she sneezed.

A cold, she thought, frowning. That's all I need! She made her way to the bathroom and looked at herself with impatience. Her face was flushed, her eyes over-bright. No doubt about it, she had a cold. It was ages since she had had one. Oh, damn! she thought. That will slow me down. It was difficult to work at full stretch when one was under the weather.

She had no appetite, so she just had orange juice and coffee for breakfast. By lunch time her sneezing had become habitual and her sore throat was making it hard to swallow.

The last thing she felt like doing was going out any-where, and she knew she would never survive a lengthy Japanese meal with all the rituals that that entailed. She had to give Simon Hilliard warning that she couldn't go. She tried to recall the name of his firm, but her mind was only operating at a subnormal level and the name escaped her. She finally decided to risk ringing Annette.

'Oh, hi,' Annette burbled happily. 'Donny and I just got back from buying the ring. It's super! What do you think? I chose an emerald, square-cut, with a diamond setting.'

'Sounds fantastic,' said Laura. 'I can't wait to see it. And it goes without saying that I send you both my best wishes.' She paused and before Annette could burst out again said: 'Look Annette, I was ringing be-cause I have to get hold of Simon Hilliard ur-gently . . .'

'What?' Annette's voice interrupted shrilly.

'Could you give me his telephone number?' Laura ploughed on bravely, disregarding the note in her sister's voice.

'My God, you've got a nerve!' Annette screeched.

'Don't scream down the phone. I've got a terrible headache,' Laura said.

'Good,' Annette spat. 'Serves you right!'

'Listen, I'm supposed to be having dinner with him . . .'

'What? What?'

'And I've got a terrible cold. I can't go, so I must ring and warn him.'

'Well!' Annette muttered, too livid to speak coherently.

'So if you could give me his number, please?'

'Get lost!' Annette snapped, hanging up so violently that Laura's eardrum was almost shattered.

She surveyed the dead phone with a grim expression before replacing it. Well, it was worth trying. What now? She put a hand to her throbbing head. Ring her father? He might know. No, she decided, not very wise. He would be as angry as Annette, for different reasons. She would just have to wait until Simon arrived and break the tidings to him on the doorstep. At least if he arrived and saw her he would know she wasn't lying to him.

She looked into the mirror at ten to seven with the intention of doing something to her face to make her look less like death warmed over, but decided to leave herself looking white and pin-eyed. At least Simon Hilliard would take one look and be quite glad she was backing out. No man could want to escort something looking like that.

He arrived promptly. Laura opened the door, huddled in a thick blue fisherman's sweater and warm cord trousers, and he stared at her in surprised assessment.

'Sorry,' she croaked. 'I can't come—I've got a cold.'

'So I hear,' he said, smiling at her. 'You sound like a frog.'

'I feel like one. Sorry.'

'It isn't your fault,' he soothed. 'Unless of course you caught a cold deliberately.'

'Oh, yes, I went down to the shops and bought one this morning,' Laura muttered, sneezing irritably.

Simon laughed, his green eyes full of wry amusement. 'Even being ill doesn't shut you up, does it?'

She looked at him drily. He was in a smooth dark suit which enhanced those good looks and made him look taller and more elegant than ever. The sight of him made her feel even more like something washed up on a beach. He really was ridiculously attractive—and far too aware of it.

'Sorry, but you'd better get going, hadn't you, or you'll be late,' she said, starting to close the door.

He did that clever trick again, inserting himself into the flat before she had a chance to shut him out, and smiling at her in kindly indulgence.

'What you need is a hot lemon with whisky.'

'I hate colds, they make me feel ghastly,' she said, sneezing again.

'They make you look ghastly,' he informed her without tact. 'It's your colouring, I suppose. When you're pale you look like a ghost.'

'Thanks, that makes me feel much better,' Laura muttered. 'Don't let me detain you, Mr Hilliard.'

'You're not detaining me. I'm going to get you a hot drink and see you into bed.'

Laura stiffened and glared at him. 'You are not!'

He laughed under his breath. 'That woke you up, didn't it? You aren't on your last legs yet.'

She snatched open the door again and looked at him

pointedly. 'Apologise to Yashi and his wife for me, would you? I'm really very sorry to have missed seeing *them*.'

His green eyes registered the point, gleaming with half impatient amusement. 'If you didn't have a cold, I'd kiss you to teach you a lesson,' he said, and then, as she abruptly moved back a step or two, 'Don't worry. I don't want to catch your cold, so I won't, but I'll bear it in mind when you're back to health.'

'Please,' Laura said sweetly, 'don't bother on my account.'

He eyed her, his mouth curling in ironic apprecia-tion. 'It will be no bother.' There was mocking inso-lence in the green eyes. 'When you haven't got a rotten cold you can be quite fetching.'

Laura's teeth snapped together. He laughed and sauntered out of the door. Laura slammed it. When she went into her bedroom a moment later and looked at herself in the mirror her high colour was not entirely due to her cold, and she was furious with her-self for letting Simon Hilliard raise her temperature with one of his teasing remarks. She should know better, she told herself, but her blue eyes were faintly evasive as she turned away from her own reflection, and as she curled up in bed later, a hotwater bottle on her icy feet, she was irritated to find herself still think-ing about the way his green eyes could tease and smile at the same time. I don't like him, she told herself. I don't. And then asked herself irritably why she felt it necessary to underline the fact.

CHAPTER FIVE

LAURA was still in bed next morning when the door-bell went. Groaning, she clambered out of bed and pulled on her dressing gown. Her cold was slightly better today, the worst of it passed. Her throat was less painful and her head no longer ached.

She opened the door and peered warily through a crack. Annette peered back. 'It's not Jack the Ripper.'

Laura opened the door to let her in, giving her a dim smile. 'Sorry, I'm in my dressing gown. It might have been the milkman.'

'So you really have got a cold,' said Annette, keeping well away. 'Don't give it to me.'

'I won't,' Laura promised. 'You'd better not stay, in case.'

'Did you go out with Simon?' Annette's smile was sharp and feline.

'No.' Laura walked towards the kitchen. 'I'm going to have a long, cool drink. My throat is dry.'

'I'm sorry if you aren't well, but I came to give you a piece of my mind,' Annette told her sharply.

'I shouldn't. You need it more than I do.'

Digesting this, Annette laughed nastily. 'You think you're a scream, don't you?'

Laura got herself some lemon barley water, offered Annette some and was given a grimace of refusal. 'Look,' she said, 'I'm feeling one degree under. Don't pick quarrels with me until I'm strong enough to listen.'

'What a nerve!' Annette sneered. 'You handed me a lot of advice about Simon.'

'Not me,' Laura denied. 'All I did was advise you to get a bottle of Patou out of it if you let him whisk you off to bed in Paris.'

'And that was charming,' Annette fumed. 'A fine sister you are!'

'What did you want me to do? Faint from shock? As you rightly said, you're a big girl now.'

'You didn't really want me to go, though, did you?' Annette gave her a smile of low cunning. 'I'm not stupid. You're the old-fashioned type. You were horrified.'

'If you say so.' Laura drank her lemon barley water slowly, the coolness of it refreshing as it slid down her dry throat.

'Then why are you dating him yourself?'

'I'm not.'

'You said . . .'

'He has a Japanese friend who invited me to meet his wife. It wasn't what I'd call a date with Simon Hilliard. And anyway, I didn't go.'

Annette's sharp eyes shifted thoughtfully. 'He isn't your type, you know.'

'He isn't anybody's type. Not if they have any sense.'

'He's probably furious with me,' said Annette, giggling. 'We had a date and I didn't show up.'

'So he said.'

Annette gave her another quick look. 'What else did he say?'

'Nothing much.'

'Wait until he hears about me and Donald.' That reminded her and she flashed an enormous emerald under Laura's dazzled eyes. 'Like it?'

'Who wouldn't?' Laura inspected it with awed admiration. 'If it was any bigger you'd never be able to lift your hand.'

'Donald's very generous,' added Annette. .

'Have you told Father?'

Annette smiled coyly. 'Yes. He was delighted.'

'I bet he was.' Laura shivered. 'Look, I'm sorry, but I do feel terrible. Mind if I go back to bed?'

Annette trailed after her. 'How come you got this invitation from Simon's Japanese friend, anyway?' she asked, returning to the attack.

'Chance,' said Laura, getting back into bed. 'Let yourself out, will you?'

'I believe you fancy him,' Annette muttered, glaring at her. 'You're crazy if you do.'

'I believe you,' Laura agreed. 'But I don't. He's the last man in the world I would want to get involved with.'

'You couldn't cope with him,' said Annette, running a hand through her full bright hair. 'You just aren't sophisticated enough.'

Laura closed her eyes. 'Goodbye.'

She heard Annette departing in something of a temper and relaxed under her covers. Apart from her cold, her problems were all over. Annette was safely engaged to Donald and their father would withdraw again to his business world, leaving Laura to get on with her own life uninterrupted. Once she had got rid of this cold, she thought, sneezing again.

She was deeply asleep that evening when someone rang the doorbell. She lifted her head, eyes flickering in dazed surprise, then lay down again and ignored the ringing. After a moment it stopped and she drifted back to sleep, not even caring to know who it had been at the door. All she wanted to do was sleep.

Next morning she felt so well she got up, took a warm shower and got dressed before eating a comparatively hearty breakfast. She was due to lunch with Declan, so she had chosen one of her favourite dresses, a dark blue sheath which moulded her slim figure and deepened the blue of her eyes. She made up very carefully before leaving to meet him. The traces of pallor which her cold had left were easily dealt with, but her nose was a trifle pink and her eyes had a faint shadow underneath them.

She took a taxi to the restaurant. Declan was late, which didn't surprise her, since he lived in a permanent state of haste which always left him several minutes behind time with everything he did.

She sat at the table watching the other guests, sipping a dry Martini, and hoping she looked almost human today.

A movement at the other side of the room caught her eye, and she glanced in that direction and saw Simon Hilliard at a table with three other men. He was in the act of rising, his eyes fixed on her, and she realised that he was coming over to speak to her, but at that second Declan blew into the restaurant and rolled towards her like a large Welsh tank, his wild black curls blown around by the wind, his voice lilting apologetically. 'Darling, I'm sorry, I'm late again—the taxi took forever and the traffic gets worse every day.' He kissed her with enthusiasm, giving her a quick bear-hug at the same time. 'Lovely to see you, you look fantastic.'

As he sank into the chair opposite her she glanced across the room. Simon was sitting down again, but he was watching her with narrowed green eyes.

She looked away. 'How are you, Declan?'

'Busy,' he grinned. 'Thank God. What about you?'

'As I said, the book's coming along.'

The waiter appeared with the tall, red-leather-backed menus and Declan ordered drinks for them both while they studied the choice of dishes.

'What was your idea?' Laura asked as they finished ordering.

'Ah,' said Declan, beginning to beam. 'You remember when you started working for us you wanted to do fiction and I got you sidetracked on to factual books? How do you feel about doing a switch again? I've got a lovely man who writes super stories, but I can't find an artist to come up with artwork to match. Then I had a brainwave. What about you?'

Rather taken aback, Laura queried: 'Just artwork? I'd never considered doing that.'

'Think about it. I could set up a lunch, give you a chance to meet this chap. You'll like him, he's fun. He's a schoolmaster with a sense of humour and his stories are a hoot. Pity he can't do the artwork himself—he'd make a fantastic job of it. His stories really need the right illustrations.'

They discussed the idea over Florida cocktail, Dover sole and a rather over-bland lemon mousse. Declan's lilting Welsh voice rose and fell excitedly, he leaned towards her, his broad shoulders hunched forward and his curly black head permanently shifting as he gestured. Declan used his whole body when he spoke, every word underlined with a movement. He was always given to sudden enthusiasms, his imagination racing away with him, especially under the influence of a good lunch accompanied by good wine. He had been drinking most of the wine they had had with their meal and his face was very flushed.

'I'll get in touch with Henry, then, and set up a working lunch,' he promised as they were served with their coffee. 'In the meantime I'll let you have the text of his book and you can see what you think.'

'How soon would you want me to start work if I agree to do the artwork?' she asked dubiously. 'Don't forget I've still got quite a lot of work to do on the birds.'

Declan gave one of his sweeping shrugs, almost knocking his coffee off the table. 'No hurry, no hurry.'

'No publication date fixed yet?' Laura asked suspiciously.

He looked shifty. 'Well——' he began.

'I thought so,' Laura sighed. 'Declan, I'm not a machine. I can't do both jobs at once.'

'Plenty of time,' he soothed, offering her a plate of Turkish delight. 'Good stuff this—have some. The real thing. Usually it's gummy rubbish, but this is genuine, melts in the mouth.'

'No, thank you,' Laura refused, looking at it without enthusiasm.

Declan popped some into his mouth. 'Silly girl! You're far too thin.' He returned to his subject, picking up her hand and smoothing out the back of it absently. 'I'm in a bit of a hole about this, Laura. We had someone fixed up for it, but when his stuff came in it was hopeless, right off the point. Henry needs someone who understands his humour and this stuff had no life in it. So we're desperately in need of the right artist.'

'Why didn't you say so?' Laura looked at her hand and hoped there would still be some of it left when he had finished. 'All the same, I can't start on it just yet.'

'How soon do you think?' Declan was sparkling again, the pathetic wheedling look leaving his face now that she was giving in.

'I'll think about it.'

He stroked her hand gratefully. 'Sweetie, I love you!'

'Can I have my hand back soon?' she grinned. 'I shall need it if I'm going to work this hard.'

He patted it. 'You've saved my life.'

'I shall expect to be well paid,' she said, and saw wary lights start up in his hazel eyes.

'Ah—um,' he began, stuffing some more Turkish delight in quickly.

'Very well paid,' Laura underlined.

Declan made gestures towards his mouth, indicating that he could not speak.

Laura grinned at him. 'Snake!'

Declan hurriedly signalled the waiter for the bill and made a big show of being totally occupied with that. When he put a hand under her elbow to guide her out of the restaurant he was talking with vital enthusiasm about a film he had just seen. He insisted on telling her the plot frame by frame all the way back to her flat, just in case she brought up the subject of money again. When they arrived he kissed her and almost threw her out of the taxi before she knew what was happening.

Wryly, Laura watched the taxi shoot away. She had the feeling Declan was pushing it.

There was a huge bouquet of flowers leaning up against her door. She stopped dead, astonished, then picked them up and extracted the card. It was from Yashi, expressing sympathy with her illness and saying how much he regretted that his wife had not been able to meet her. He was going back to Japan at once, he went on, but he hoped there would be another chance for his wife to meet her at some later date.

Laura was rather touched by his concern and kindness. They had only met so briefly. It was a very kind gesture.

She spent some time arranging the flowers in the biggest vase she owned, a huge blue glazed object which she liked to use in still lifes because the blue was such a lovely deep shade.

She was just carrying it out of the kitchen when the doorbell went. Laura automatically went to open it, still clutching the vase, and then realised that she had a small problem. Juggling the vase in one arm, she opened the door and then peered through a mass of tall-stemmed gladioli.

'Is that a disguise or a shield?' Simon Hilliard asked her with polite amusement.

'Yashi sent them.' Laura stood in the doorway, shifting the vase so that she could see him better. 'It was very nice of him.'

'He's a very nice man. They look rather heavy. Allow me.' Simon removed the vase deftly and walked off with it into the flat. Laura wrathfully slammed the door and followed, eyeing the back of his black head with extreme indignation.

'I don't recall asking you in.'

'Where shall I put them?' He stood in her sitting-room, looking around with a thoughtful expression. 'Over by the window, don't you think?' He carried them over and put them on a small low table. The vivid blooms immediately gave the window a new appeal, the blue sky behind them making the whole room look brighter. 'There, that looks fine,' said Simon, stepping back to admire the effect.

'What are you doing here?' Laura enquired.

'Who was that having lunch with you?' He swung round and his green eyes fixed her intently.

Laura flushed a little. 'A friend.'

'One of the hand-holding variety,' he commented. 'Obviously a close friendship. You seemed to have a lot to say to each other.'

'Yes,' Laura said coldly, 'we did.' Had he been watching them all through lunch? What right did he think he had to come here asking pointed questions?

'Have dinner with me,' he said, still staring at her, the yellow threads in his cat-like eyes very bright.

'That's very polite of you, but . . .' she began.

'Your cold is obviously better,' he pointed out before she could make that an excuse.

'I have a date,' Laura lied, smiling sweetly.

He didn't believe her. She caught the narrowing of his eyes and knew he was aware she was lying, but her sweet smile stayed pinned on her face.

'Lunch tomorrow,' he said.

'Of course I'd love to, but I'm afraid . . .' She shrugged, still smiling.

'Okay,' he said with a smile which was as unreal as her own but which had temper behind it. 'When are you free? We'll do it that way, shall we? You name the time and place.'

Laura's lashes flickered as she looked down, thinking hard. He had caught her there. Looking up again, she resumed her smile. 'I'm afraid I'm not—free, I mean. For dates with people, that is. I'm fully booked.'

'With the man from lunch?' he said slowly.

She nodded, shrugging. 'Sorry, but there you are.' Her blue eyes very wide, she smiled at him again. 'But it's very nice of you to ask.'

'Isn't it?' he asked cryptically, taking a step which brought him far too close to her. With a startled, apprehensive look Laura said: 'What?'

He laughed at the upward flicker of her glance. His hands shot out and caught her face, held it tilted towards him.

'Let go!' Laura exclaimed, colour running up her cheeks. She tried to pull away, but he wouldn't let her. Off balance, she grabbed instinctively at him to stop herself from falling, a peculiar sensation of alarmed confusion widening her eyes and making her breathe fast.

'I've promised mylf this ever since we met,' he said, bending down towards her.

She looked into the mocking green eyes for a few seconds before her eyes dropped involuntarily to the hard, sensual outline of his mouth. Time seemed to stand still as it came closer. Laura felt her heart pick up and begin to race as though she were under the threat of some unknown danger. Her fingers tightened on his shoulders and then his mouth touched her own. For the first moment the contact was light and warm, then one of his hands moved and pressed her towards him, hard against her yielding spine, and the kiss took fire, his mouth burning a demand into hers which she knew she was helplessly satisfying.

Simon's fingers moved over the back of her head, twisting into her hair, and Laura clung to his wide shoulders, her head flung back under the increasingly passionate pressure of his mouth. A heavy silence seemed to shut them in together, the mindless movements of their bodies fevered. Laura ran her arms around his neck and swayed closer, intensely absorbed in the sheer physical pleasure he was giving.

When at last he lifted his head she was shaking, her body weak, her head spinning. She opened her eyes and looked at him in dazed disbelief. It had never happened to her before. No man had ever made her feel like that; she wasn't sure she liked it.

Simon was breathing thickly, his face flushed. 'Yes,' he said in a deep, husky voice.

Laura wasn't sure her voice worked. She tried it, hesitantly. 'Yes, what?' Relieved to find a sound emerged, she tried a brittle little smile to go with it, hoping it would cover her complete confusion.

'I like it,' said Simon, and moved towards her again.

Laura panicked. She wriggled out of his grip with a determination which succeeded in freeing her from his hands and fled across the room to stand behind a chair. 'Oh, no,' she said, swallowing, facing him like a frightened animal at bay. 'Not me you don't, Mr Hilliard. I'm not my sister. I'm sorry if you haven't got anyone to take to Paris, but you can always scout around on the spot.'

'So I can,' he murmured, making no attempt to pursue her, his green eyes hard and watchful now. 'Tell me, how did you talk Annette out of it?'

'Told her about your bet.'

'Ah,' he said, smiling tightly. 'Clever stuff.'

'Have you heard she just got engaged to Donald?' Laura smiled at him, relieved to find her heart had stopped thudding like a steamhammer.

'She rang me to give me the good news,' he said, surprising her.

She wasn't sure she liked that. Why had Annette done that?

He read her thoughts and gave her a mocking little smile. 'Your sister is one of those who likes to have her cake and eat it.'

Oh, dear, Laura thought, frowning. What was Annette up to now? Surely she wasn't stupid enough to get involved with him again after discovering the sort of man he was?

'You both have a lot of your father in you,' said Simon with a hard glinting look in the green eyes.

'You aren't very keen on my father, are you?' Laura studied him, wondering again what it was that made him look so icy whenever he mentioned her father.

'I told you, I detest him.'

'Why?'

Simon's mouth twisted in crooked distate. 'It's a long story and not a very pretty one. Have you asked him?'

'No and if I did I doubt if he would tell me,' Laura admitted frankly.

'I doubt it, too,' he drawled. 'In fact I'd lay money on it that he'd die rather than tell you about it.'

Her brows creased and she looked at him in anxious concern. 'Is it that bad? Something my father did? Business?'

'Not business,' he said, and she had a curious suspicion that he was hesitating about telling her the truth. 'Maybe I'll tell you one day.' He turned towards the door. 'But as you refuse to have dinner with me I suppose that only leaves Annette.'

'She just got engaged!'

He swung, one hand in his pocket, a cynical smile on his lips. 'My God, you're naïve!'

Very flushed, Laura snapped angrily: 'You may not think a little thing like an engagement matters, but I think it does! And so will Donald. Annette shouldn't see other men now. She's given Donald her word.'

He regarded her with wry amusement. 'It isn't me you should be convincing, it's your sister. I didn't ring her, she rang me.'

'To tell you she was marrying Donald!'

'If you say that often enough you might convince yourself, but you'll never convince me,' he drawled.

'Doesn't it bother you that Donald adores her and you could hurt him?'

'If it doesn't bother Annette, I fail to see why it should bother me. I'm not engaged to the fellow; she is. Either she cares for him or she doesn't. That's no business of mine.'

'So it won't worry you if you break up her engagement?'

He gave a long, deliberate sigh, his shoulders lifting in a shrug. 'If the engagement meant a damned thing I couldn't do it any harm. If Annette loved him she wouldn't consider a date with me.' His eyes held hers, mockery in them. 'Now would she?'

Laura didn't answer. She looked at him with acute dislike. It would be very satisfying to be able to fling back his arguments, but to her fury she had to see the justice of his case. Annette didn't love Donald and there was no way round that.

Simon waited, smiling, then said softly: 'Want to reconsider your own answer? Will you have dinner with me?'

Laura lifted her head, her blue eyes cold. 'Get lost! You're not blackmailing me. If my sister is fool enough to run around with you at the risk of breaking her engagement, that's her lookout.'

She caught a flash of surprise in the green eyes, a twist of his mouth. He had expected her to cave in under his threat of dating Annette, she realised. Well, he was wrong. She wasn't doing anything of the sort.

He turned away. Laura calmly walked after him to the front door. He looked down at her, his face quizzical. 'I suppose I'm to gather from that that the fellow you had lunch with really matters to you?'

Laura couldn't help the quick, involuntary smile that came at this idea of Declan. Friend though he was, there had never been anything more than friendship between them, and it amused her to have him believed to be her lover. 'Yes,' she said gravely, eyes lowered to hide the smile in them.

There was a brief silence. She looked up through her lashes. Simon stared at her, the usual teasing amusement absent from his face and a harsh frown drawing his black brows together.

'Lucky man,' he said, before walking away.

It occurred to Laura to ring Annette and give her a lecture on being faithful to Donald now that she had given her word to him, but she dismissed that idea as a pointless waste of time and probably counter-productive into the bargain. It didn't fail to dawn on her that she might have precipitated Annette's phone call to Simon, anyway, by telling her sister that she had a dinner date with him. Annette's dog-in-the-manger tendencies would have come out in her when she contemplated the picture of Laura with Simon. Ringing Annette had been a stupid mistake, one she would never have made if she hadn't been feeling rotten. She wouldn't compound her folly by letting Annette think that it would upset her to know that Annette was chasing Simon again. It was far wiser to ignore the whole thing.

Two days later she had lunch with her father. It had surprised her to get another call from him. She had somehow imagined he would forget her very existence again now that Annette was safely, as he supposed, engaged to Donald.

He gave her his usual brusque kiss, brushing his lips over her cheek, before summoning the waiter to order an aperitif. As they sipped their drinks and studied the menu, he said: 'I've just been to see a doctor.'

Laura looked up, startled by the abrupt statement. 'Is anything wrong?'

George Sloane's pale blue eyes met hers directly and without any sign of emotion. 'Yes.'

The staccato word increased her alarm, and she put down the menu. 'What is it, Father?' For the first time she felt a deep regret for their long inability to communicate, for the gulf between them which she had never tried to bridge. Her father had always been so self-sufficient; a cold, withdrawn man obsessed by his own world and indifferent to everything but business. Laura had learnt to live as though her father meant no more to her than a chance-met stranger, but George Sloane was not a stranger, he was her father, and she looked at him with disturbed awareness of that fact.

'I've got to have an operation.' He glanced at her menu. 'Well, have you decided what you're going to have?' There was irritation in the question and she automatically picked up her menu again and looked at it blindly.

'What's wrong with you?' The words on the menu made no sense to her. She shut it again and looked at him.

He ran one hand over his thinning hair, his face blank. 'Heart.' Glancing around, he said tersely: 'Where's that waiter?'

The waiter appeared, catching the impatient glare of those cold blue eyes, and George Sloane ordered. When the man had gone again he looked round at Laura, who was wishing he would make it easier for her to cope with the situation. Even at a moment like this, her father handed off all human contact with that icy stare.

'I've got a fifty-fifty chance, they tell me.' His smooth-skinned face bore no sign of fear or anxiety. 'I could have wished for better odds than that.'

It was a joke, Laura realised, belatedly, and smiled, her lips trembling slightly.

'I'm sure . . .'

Her father didn't let her finish that sentence, reading her uncertain attempt at reassurance and dismissing it out of hand. 'I'll have the best available heart surgeon. I'm taking no chances.' He refused to accept her comfort, she saw. He preferred to rely on the hard fact of his own assessment of the situation.

She tried again, reaching a hand across the table, her palm turned upward in a pleading little gesture. 'I'm very sorry, Father. Is there anything I can do?'

George Sloane looked at her hand as though not sure what to do about it, then touched it briefly, patting it. 'There's one thing. If anything happens to me, make sure Annette marries Donald.'

Laura almost laughed. 'Yes, I will,' she promised, and didn't add, as she was tempted to do, 'If I can,' because he did not want the truth at the moment. He wanted to feel secure about Annette. Perhaps, in his own cold way, he genuinely cared for her as he did not care for any of the rest of them. Or was it still only his company which he was protecting? Was he so scared of Simon Hilliard that even faced with the possibility of death he was obsessed with a desire to keep his company safe from him?

'Whatever happens, she mustn't marry Hilliard,' her father said. 'That would be disastrous.'

'I don't think he's the marrying kind,' Laura pointed out.

George Sloane's pale lips twisted. 'To get his hands on my firm he'd marry the devil himself.'

A nice comparison, Laura thought, glancing away. She looked back guardedly, watching her father's face. 'Why does he dislike you so much, Father?'

A faint flush came into the pale face. 'What?' She caught the wary flicker of his eyes.

'He hates you, doesn't he?'

George Sloane hesitated. Laura waited, silently urging him to confide in her, hoping that he would break the wall of silence which had stood between them all her life and make some sort of contact at last.

But he lowered his eyes, fiddling with his glass. 'We never did get on,' he said evasively, and she realised that he wasn't going to give her any insight into what went on behind that bland cold mask of a face.

'When are you going to have the operation?'

'A couple of week's time,' he said as though he was talking about some minor matter. The waiter arrived with their first course. 'Ah, the salmon,' said George with a faint sign of enthusiasm, and from that moment onward he refused to discuss the subject of his operation.

As he was putting her into a taxi afterwards, though,

he did say curtly: 'Don't mention the operation to anyone, will you?'

Laura looked at him in surprise. 'You're telling Annette and Philip, though?'

'No,' he said, and at her exclamation of disbelief, frowned. 'Laura, the last thing I want is word of this to get around. If Hilliard heard I was ill he'd move in for the kill. He's been buying stock already. He hasn't got much, but if it was known that I wasn't in the best of health the price of shares would slump overnight. Hilliard could pick up quite a few at a low price, and I'm not risking anything of the sort.'

'But, Father . . .'

'I'm serious,' he said with a direct, commanding stare. 'Annette can't keep secrets. The whole of London would know in five minutes.'

'But what about Philip? He'll have to know.'

'I'll tell him I'm going abroad for a few weeks. My secretary can be trusted. She's been with me for years. If anything happens she can deal with it.'

Laura was horrified. It wasn't fair to Philip and Annette to keep them in the dark about the gravity of his illness. She looked at him in anxious concern. 'Father, I really think you must tell them. What if anything happened?'

'If I don't survive the operation it will be too late for them to cause any problems,' he said, horrifying her even more.

'Never mind the company, Father. They're your children! They have a right to know you're seriously ill. What will they feel like when they realise you didn't even tell them?'

He looked into her eyes with an odd, wry smile. 'Annette hasn't got much feeling. She'll cry a bit, but she'll get over it. Philip . . .' He shrugged. 'It would scare him rigid to be told. He couldn't cope with it. No, best to keep it quiet and see how it comes out.' He closed the taxi door and stood back, giving the driver her address.

Laura drove away feeling chilled and distressed. She was half impressed by her father's courage and honesty about his situation, half disturbed by his lack of any wish for human comfort at such a moment. It seemed an inhuman way to face the possibility of death, but perhaps that was the only way he could face it. He was facing death as he had faced life—alone. Laura did not envy him, but she admired him in a reluctant, appalled fashion.

CHAPTER SIX

BACK at her flat Laura sat listening to a slow whisper of rain running down the window, her face disturbed. Why had her father rung her, told her, when he had refused to tell Annette and Philip? Had he wanted to make some sort of contact, after all? Yet when she tried to express her sympathy, her concern, he had pushed both away with a cold expression. Laura found it impossible to understand him.

She rarely saw her brother and his wife. Pleasant enough though they both were, they just weren't on her wavelength and conversation with them always ground to a halt. Daphne's interests were so limited. She could talk about her newest electronic gadget, her hair-style, her latest dinner party, but beyond that she seemed to have little interest in anything. She meant well, that much one could say about her. Laura often felt there was nothing of Daphne one could not see and hear. Alone, she might well cease to exist, like a switched-off android.

Philip was real enough. Nervous, worried, vaguely hopeless, he had lived for too long in his father's shadow. Laura was afraid that their father was quite right in suspecting that if Simon Hilliard decided to try to take over the firm Philip would offer him very little real opposition.

What lay behind the hatred which existed between Simon and her father? she wondered. She was certain that her father had briefly hesitated before refusing to tell her. What had he done which made him so reluctant to talk about it? Did Simon have some sort of blackmail hold over him?

No, she thought, not that, or, from what she knew of Simon, he might well have used it by now.

There was something, though, something which changed the expression in both men's eyes when they came near to talking about it. Simon Hilliard's usual expression was one of teasing mockery, but when he spoke of her father his green eyes became hard and icy. When her father talked about Simon, he looked apprehensive, almost frightened, his obvious dislike always accompanied by that silent fear.

What on earth could her father have done? Laura was under no illusions about George Sloane's capacity for cold, ruthless selfishness. She had seen it practised against her mother; she had had it revealed to herself. It wouldn't surprise Laura to be told that her father had done something which could be used as a threat against him.

Getting up on impulse, she rang Daphne and invited her and Philip to dinner the next night. Daphne consulted her diary. 'Oh, we'd have loved to, but we're having dinner with the Faronsons. What a pity.' She made the correct noises without conveying any sense of meaning them.

'Some other night?' Laura suggested.

'Oh, lovely,' said Daphne, cooing.

They fixed a date and Laura rang off. Of course, she couldn't tell them about the operation, but she might be able to find out from Philip exactly how things stood in the firm, whether her father had any good reason for his obvious anxiety over Simon Hilliard. It wouldn't be easy to pump Philip, not because he would be reluctant to talk, but because he wouldn't understand what it was she was trying to find out and might not even know very much more than she did. Philip could be incredibly dense about things.

The rain had stopped. Laura stood at the window looking into the night, watching the ceaseless movements of the sky, windblown clouds drifting in ragged procession across a sickle-shaped moon. A restless impatience possessed her and she felt oddly ill at ease. She wanted to get out of this quiet flat; walk, keep walking, as though only to be on the move could quieten the nagging thoughts which were disturbing her mind.

Snatching up a jacket, she went out and walked down towards the steep streets of Hampstead. The lightless area of the Heath breathed softly, trees rustling in the wind, but the traffic was still quite heavy at this hour of the evening, streaming in and out of London, and above the artery of London roads glowed the orange street lamps.

Laura had some vague intention of stopping in Hampstead to get a cup of coffee. It gave a purpose to her otherwise aimless walk. But as she made her way down towards the tube station a car pulled up beside her.

She gave it a startled, apprehensive look. Cars which stopped at night around here were not usually driven by anyone familiar. She edged away, stiffening.

The passenger door swung open and someone leaned across from the driver's seat. Laura couldn't see his face, but she got an impression of someone very tall and dark. Giving him a quick, nervous look, she began to walk away fast.

She heard a door slam, quick footsteps following her. Oh, no! she thought, starting to run. It was ridiculous to be frightened. This was a busy road; cars were speeding past all the time, the street lights blazed overhead. Laura knew it was absurd to feel panic surging into her, but she did.

The sound of running feet came closer and then a hand seized her shoulder. Laura looked round, breathing fast, her heart in her throat.

'What the hell are you doing?'

'Oh!' she gasped, so relieved she felt sick. 'It's you!' Her tense muscles relaxed for a few seconds before she got annoyed. Pink ran up her face and she glared at him. 'You scared the living daylights out of me!'

He had been frowning blackly, his face drawn into angry lines, but at her muttered words he began to laugh, his features softening.

'Thought I was a cruising gentleman trying to pick you up, did you?'

'It isn't funny!'

'You can't see your face!'

'I was petrified!' Her heart was still pounding against her breastbone and her legs felt as weak as water.

Simon smiled at her mockingly. 'Serves you right, wandering around the streets alone at this hour!'

'It isn't that late!'

'Then why were you so scared?'

Laura didn't want to be reminded of her brief moment of panic. It had been a hairy experience and her nerves were still jangling from it. 'Oh, go away,' she said, trying to pull free of his hand.

It tightened on her shoulderbone and she looked up at him in indignation.

'Let go!'

He was a good head taller than herself, the long lean body far too masculine and, although he was so slim, far too powerful. Laura was very glad he hadn't been the insistent stranger she had thought he was for a moment. She wouldn't have had a chance. There was something very scaring about the idea of struggling with a stranger. You knew you couldn't try to talk them out of it, and when you were as small and physically weak as Laura you knew you couldn't win a fight. Although Simon didn't frighten her like that she was angry with him for having given her such a scare.

'I'll drive you home,' he said, still looking amused, as though her fit of fury was a joke.

Laura measured him with a cold eye. 'No, thank you. I'm perfectly capable of looking after myself.'

'So I saw,' he mocked, his eyes very bright. She could see it was giving him a lot of pleasure to have seen her scared out of her wits, and that made her even angrier.

'Would you mind letting go of my shoulder?' she asked with a dignified courtesy which had the sting of rage behind it.

He regarded her, his mouth twitching. 'I like you much better when that cool little face isn't quite so cool,' he observed. 'You can be quite human when the mask slips.' His eyes dropped to her mouth, reminding her silently of the last time they met, and Laura felt hot, betraying colour rush up her face.

Through clenched teeth she said: 'You'll find out how human I am if you don't let me go. I'll kick you so hard you'll be limping for days!'

'Temper, temper,' he mocked, grinning. 'How's the book coming along? Drawn any good birds lately?'

Laura had never had any trouble containing her temper before. She wasn't going to lose it now, she decided. She counted to ten, her eyes lowered, and assumed a false smile.

'My book is fine, thank you.'

'Why are you walking around here at night? Something bothering you?'

She looked up, startled. 'No,' she lied, but there had been a brief hesitation before she spoke and she was afraid he might have picked that up. 'I like to walk at night when I'm at work on a book.'

'A risky habit,' he advised. 'I should drop it if I were you. Next time it might not be someone you know who stops his car.'

'I'll bear it in mind,' Laura promised.

'Do that,' he said, laughing softly at her limpid expression, the meekness belied by a sharpness in the wide blue eyes.

'What are you doing in Hampstead, anyway?' Laura asked. 'Do you live around here?'

'No, I was on my way to see Annette.'

Laura looked at him, her face hardening. 'Oh, were you?'

'Yes,' he mocked, his mouth curling. 'But since I've met you, why don't we have a drink and talk it over?'

'Talk what over?' Laura asked, thinking fast behind her pretence of a smile. He was on his way to see Annette, was he? For some reason she hadn't seriously believed he would go on seeing her sister now that Annette was engaged to Donald. She had believed that to be a blackmail threat which he wouldn't carry out if she called his bluff.

'I'll think of something,' said Simon, watching her intently. 'How about the latest world news? Or whether the polar ice-cap is melting?'

Laura viewed him with disfavour. If he ruined Annette's engagement at this moment it could seriously upset her father and even damage his chances of surviving that operation.

'Coming?' Simon enquired. She had the feeling he expected her to say no, but she gave him a saccharine smile and said: 'Thank you, I'd like that.'

She caught a flash of surprise in his eyes, but he didn't comment on her sudden change of mind until they were in his car and driving away. Then he said: 'Why the sudden turn-around? Or did the compelling charm of my personality dawn on you at last?'

'That would be it,' Laura agreed solemnly.

He gave her a hard stare. 'Why did you really change your mind?'

'I thought we'd agreed that it was all your compelling charm?' she asked as he shot round a corner and parked outside one of Hampstead's most popular pubs.

He switched off the engine and turned to face her, his eyes cool and penetrating. 'I've an idea you're a dangerous female. Behind that pair of big blue eyes there's a brain.'

'Thank you,' Laura said gratefully.

He grinned. 'I don't trust you an inch.'

'That's funny,' she said, fluttering her eyelashes at him. 'I don't trust you either.'

'I'd say there was common ground there,' he observed. 'We may not trust each other, but at least we have some measure of understanding.'

'Why should we want that?' Laura enquired.

'It gives us something to talk about over dinner,' he said, getting out of the car.

As she joined him Laura asked: 'Dinner? Who said anything about dinner? A drink, you said.'

'That's now,' Simon agreed. 'Tomorrow night it's dinner.'

'You go too fast.'

'I've got a feeling I'm going to have to,' he said, steering her into the pub, 'before you change that mind of yours again.'

The bar was quite crowded, but they managed to find a corner table and sat down with their drinks under a large framed copy of an old *London Gazette* newspaper that had black headlines about a Victorian murder screaming across the yellowed paper.

'Tell me about your work,' he invited, leaning back to watch her face with a flicker of curiosity in his eyes.

'Tell you what?'

'How did you start doing it?'

She briefly told him about Declan and he asked some more questions, some of them so quick and casual that she barely thought about them before answering, and it was something of a shock when he asked her: 'Declan? An odd name. Not a common name at all.'

Laura looked at him in surprise. 'No, it isn't.'

'You're unlikely to know two people called Declan,' he said.

She sat upright, her eyes widening.

'I heard you call the man you had lunch with the other day Declan,' he said softly.

Laura's mind worked like greased lightning. 'Yes, that's right,' she agreed in an unruffled tone. 'That's Declan.'

'Your publisher,' he said, smiling.

'Among other things.'

They stared at each other and she refused to give a sign of realising what he meant.

'I see,' he said, still trying to read her thoughts. He looked at his glass and drank the rest of his drink. 'Can I get you another one of those?'

'No, thank you,' Laura refused, glancing at her watch. 'I must be going, I'm afraid.'

He didn't argue. As they drove to her flat he was silent, his eyes on the road and his head averted from her. Laura wondered what he was thinking about. Whatever was in his mind, he wasn't enjoying the thought; his black brows almost met across his forehead.

'Are you going to ask me in for a cup of coffee?' he asked as he parked outside her flat.

Laura hesitated. Normally when a date brought her home, that was just what she would do, but she wasn't sure she could handle Simon Hilliard. Or was the truth that she wasn't sure she could handle herself where he was concerned?

'Don't rush with an invitation,' he said, sounding irritated.

'Of course, do come in,' Laura returned, trying to sound cool and offhand without being rude.

'Thank you,' he said sarcastically.

Laura had tried not to think about those moments in his arms the other day, but even as her mind skated away from the memory every time, she always felt a curious, excited tremor which was entirely new to her. She couldn't remember a man making her feel so nervous since she was a very young teenager, but although she was attracted to him she knew it wasn't wise. It seemed ironic that the first man who had ever made her heart miss a beat should also be the last man in the world she could trust. Simon Hilliard had too many reasons for wanting to get his own back on a member of the Sloane family.

Laura only wished she knew what those reasons were. She wondered how far she would get if she asked him directly, and suspected he would clam up as firmly as her father had.

While she made the coffee he prowled around her sitting-room, picking up ornaments or flicking through some of her sketchpads, glancing along her rows of books and laughing once or twice at things he found.

'You're a cartoonist,' he said as she carried the coffee through from the kitchen.

She looked at the sheaf of drawings he held. 'When I'm in the mood, but you need a special sort of mind for that and I'm not original enough.'

'You've got a sense of humour. That must be a first in the Sloane family.'

Laura didn't dispute that. How could she? One of the reasons why she found it so hard to talk to the other members of her family was that they rarely saw a joke and usually treated one as though it was a dangerous object which might explode if they went too close to it.

Most of the men she had been out with seemed to feel the same. They reacted with stung pride to any joke she made, especially when they were trying to make love to her. Humour and sex didn't seem to go together in their view.

Laura had never had to struggle for her virtue. When things got a little heated, all she had to do was laugh. It was like a cold shower, it turned men off quicker than you could whistle. Having learnt that, she had known she was quite safe with most men. Looking at Simon out of the corner of her eye as she poured the cofee, she was disturbed to recognise that her usual technique might not work with him. The trouble was, he had a sense of humour, too.

Putting down the drawings, he came over to take his coffee cup from her and sink down on the couch. Laura was intending to sit in an armchair, discretion being the better part of valour, but Simon's mocking grin made her change her mind. She sat down beside him, returning the smile calmly, as though not understanding what lay behind it.

'Your father must be over the moon now that Annette is safely on the way to marry Foulds.' He sipped his coffee, regarding her over the brim of the cup with wry sarcasm.

'He's delighted.'

'I bet he is—and Phil? Is he delighted too?'

'Philip?' Laura picked up the intimate note in his voice. 'Yes, I expect he is. I suppose you know Philip quite well. You worked with him?'

'I worked with him,' he agreed drily. 'Has his marriage worked out? Is he rapturously happy?'

The deep, harsh unamused tone surprised her. 'I'm not sure whether he's rapturous, but I think his marriage is fine.'

Simon's mouth curled. 'That's great.'

Laura was picking up vibrations which puzzled and disturbed her. She watched his face intently. His lids were drawn down over his eyes and hid their expression, but in profile the handsome features had a stony look, anger tightening them.

'Have you met Daphne?' she asked.

He laughed shortly. 'I've seen her.'

Laura was quite certain now that his anger had something to do with Philip's marriage; his voice, his taut body, made that clear. She thought in sudden disbelief: he can't have been in love with Daphne? And then bit back a smile. The idea was too absurd. Daphne? She thought of her brother's neat, complacent wife with her talk of dishwashers and the price of fish, and mentally dismissed the idea. Simon Hilliard wouldn't even look at Daphne, she was sure of that.

'More coffee?' she asked, her hand poised to lift the coffee pot.

'Thanks.' Simon handed her his cup and their eyes met. She saw the deep angry glow in his which had appeared on their first meeting when he realised she was a member of the Sloane family. It was an expression she was beginning to recognise. Simon was angry about something.

'And you?' he asked, his lips barely moving so that the words came out in a clipped way. 'Who is he going to marry you off to?'

Laura poured his coffee, her blonde head bent. 'He isn't—if you mean my father.' She handed him his cup.

He laughed unpleasantly. 'No? I'll wait and see.'

'You do that,' Laura retorted.

'I'll lay you anything you like he's picked somebody out.'

She shrugged. 'If he has, I haven't heard anything about it. And it wouldn't make any difference if he had. If I ever marry it will be a man of my own choosing.'

'I've heard that before.' The harsh tone startled her.

Eyes opening wide, she stared at him. 'What? When?'

Simon put down his cup with a little crash. 'Forget it.' Leaning back with his head against the couch, he surveyed her, the green eyes hard.

'Is this Declan the man of your choosing?'

Laura began to smile and was angry with herself for doing so, but the idea of Declan always made her smile. He was like a large, exuberant child whose energy can be exhausting but who cannot be taken seriously or ever make you angry. He had never made Laura feel anything but amused and affectionate.

'Why is that funny?' Simon demanded, his voice suddenly icy. 'Every time he comes up you start to smile.'

'Declan makes me smile.' It was safe to admit that. An adoring woman might well say something of the sort. Simon wasn't to know what manner of smile she was giving.

'Does your father approve?' He was staring at her, his eyes slits of green. 'Is that it? You know he approves of the man you've chosen?'

Laura shrugged without saying anything. It was the safest thing to do.

'I didn't get the impression you were crazy about the man,' Simon said brusquely.

'Didn't you?'

'Don't hedge,' he muttered, watching her fixedly. 'It's a simple enough question. Are you in love with him?'

Laura felt herself flushing. 'You do ask personal questions,' she said after a pause, her voice evasive.

'Try answering one.'

'Why on earth should I? What business is it of yours?'

'I hate wasting my time,' he drawled, his face

changing and a sparkle coming into the green eyes.

Laura stiffened and half began to rise, her eyes full of surprised alarm. She hadn't been expecting that sudden change of mood, her mind fully occupied in wondering what lay behind his questions about Philip. Now as she met his hard, bright stare she saw his pupils dilate, their darkness taking over the whole of the green eyes. Her pulse began to quicken in dizzy reaction.

The next second he was pulling her back against the couch, an arm around her waist, his mouth searching for her own. Laura was too shaken to take evasive measures. She felt the race of her heart grow so rapidly that as her lips parted under his fierce kiss she was half deaf with the sound of her own blood pounding in her ears.

The cool reasoning power which went hand in hand with her sense of humour had apparently left her as certainly as her ability to laugh. She had never been swamped by emotion before, and she did not know how to fight it.

Trembling, she slid her hands up his chest and clasped his neck, feeling the rigid muscular tension straining under her palms, the thick black hair brushing her fingertips and making her nerve ends prickle with excitement.

Her eyes shut, leaving her other senses free to explore this moment, sending messages along her nerves to her brain, teaching her the scent of his skin, the feel of that rough hair against her hands, the weight of his body as he lay against her, the deep beating of his heart as his kiss demanded her surrender.

It was the first time in her life that she had ever allowed feeling to take her over. Somewhere at the back of her head, she knew she was crazy. This man hated her father. In fact, she was beginning to think he hated the whole of her family, even poor harmless Philip. But as his hand slid down her body from her breast to her thigh his exploring fingers awoke pulses everywhere they touched, as though her blood flowed in their wake, attracted by their very lightest touch.

This was what she had been afraid would happen as she hesitated about asking him in for coffee. It was not his attempt to make love to her which had scared her rigid; it was her own secret desire to have him make love to her. Although she hadn't been admitting that to herself some part of her mind had known all about it. You can't hide a thing from your own subconscious. Laura hadn't been allowing herself to recognise what her body had known from the moment she met him, but now she was forced to recognise it. Simon Hilliard turned her on and whatever the consequences of her reckless response now she was too aroused to care.

He moved back, breathing jerkily. She felt him staring at her. Her lids felt too heavy to be lifted, but she forced them open to look back at him, her blue eyes drowsy and dilated.

'You really get to me,' he muttered, his voice unsteady. 'When I saw you at that party of Annette's I thought: she's as cool as a cucumber now but what does she look like when she's making love?'

Laura was struggling to pull herself together, shuddering free of the dangerous excitement still possessing her. So that was what he had been thinking, was it?

Hoping her voice would sound steadier than his did, she said drily: 'I've often wondered what men thought about—apart from cricket and football and where the next drink was coming from.'

His black lashes flickered, as though her reply surprised him, then his mouth smiled crookedly. 'Well, now you know.'

'So I do,' she agreed. 'What a charming lot you are!'

He gave a short laugh. 'I'll say this for your sex, you recover quickly.'

Laura took the point without blinking. Smiling calmly, she said: 'Oh, we bounce back.'

His brows jerked together. 'Damn you,' he muttered in sudden, harsh resentment. 'You didn't seem to be smiling much a minute ago.'

Laura assessed his face thoughtfully. She recognised that expression. She had seen it before. Simon had the familiar look of a man whose ego just got dented. So his sense of humour wasn't as strong as she had thought it might be, it seemed.

'Hard to smile much when you're being kissed,' she pointed out, her blue eyes mocking.

His face burned with dark colour. 'Hell,' he said under his breath. 'You're even more like your old man than I'd thought.'

Opening her eyes wide, Laura said: 'You haven't been kissing him?'

For a second he gazed at her blankly, then he began to laugh, his black head flung back. 'You little bitch,' he said, when he could speak. 'I wonder some desperate man hasn't strangled you before now.'

'I think it's occurred to one or two.'

'I bet.' He moved away and studied her with the curiosity of someone inspecting a strange species. 'You're an enigma. Just now I know damned well you were with me all the way, but you switch off like a machine. Not a very alluring quality.'

'Who said I wanted to be alluring?'

He moved restlessly, stretching out his long legs and contemplating his shoes as though he had never seen them before, his hands linked behind his head.

'I don't like women with brains like a computer.'

'I thought you were into computers,' Laura commented, smiling, her eyes on his face and wondering if she imagined it or if he was looking like a sulky child.

He looked up quickly, his mouth indenting, the thrust of his jawline aggressive.

'I'm not in the habit of making love to them.'

'Don't think you're getting into the habit of making love to me, either,' Laura told him.

'My God, I think I could,' he said, starting to laugh again. The angry lines of his face relaxed and the green eyes were bright and amused. 'A pity you're a Sloane.'

Laura tensed. 'Is it? Why?'

He shot her another look, his frown returning abruptly. After a pause he said: 'It isn't a breed I care for much.'

'We aren't all the same,' Laura said quietly.

'Oh, I think you have some of the characteristic markings,' Simon drawled. 'You're too damned cool-headed and you have no intention of letting your feelings get away with you, do you? You may not be as ruthless as the rest of your family, but at a pinch I suspect you'd manage to cut throats without weeping too much.'

Laura watched him. 'Whose throat has my father cut lately?'

Simon showed her his teeth in a sudden savage snarl. 'Not mine, lady. Just let him try! But he's cut a few in the past and I doubt if it keeps him awake at night.'

Laura doubted it, too. Whose throat had her father cut that had made Simon Hilliard detest him so much?

'Why are you buying shares in the firm?' she asked.

It caught him off guard. His eyes narrowed, his face tightened. 'What?' He drew a sharp breath and regarded her coolly. 'Who says I've been?'

'My father.'

'You've discussed me with him?'

'Your name came up.'

'Did it indeed?' Simon lay back, his hands pressing the back of his head, ruffling the thick black hair. 'What did he say about me?'

'He mentioned that you were buying shares.'

'And wondered what I was doing,' he said softly.

Laura gave him a dry look. 'Oh, I don't think he wondered anything of the sort. I think he had a pretty shrewd idea what you were doing.'

'Bothers him, does it?'

From the way he watched her as he asked that, Laura could tell that he hoped very much that he was bothering her father. She smiled at him politely. 'I don't think so. If you want to buy shares why should it bother him?'

He laughed curtly. 'Why, indeed?' He rose, his long body towering over her. 'It's getting late, I'd better be on my way. Thanks for the coffee and so on.' The mocking slant of his eyes underlined the last words. Laura refused to blush or look aware.

She stood up too. 'Not at all.' Her tone was even more polite, faintly frosted with her refusal to know the meaning of that mocking little smile.

'Dinner tomorrow?' he asked casually on his way to the door.

'I'm afraid I have a date,' said Laura. She wanted to

keep him away from Annette for her father's protection, but tonight she had been forced to realise that self-protection came first. She might have recovered quite quickly from those kisses, but she knew how close she had come to the edge of oblivion. Simon Hilliard was dangerous to her. She wasn't giving him any more chances to send her crazy.

'Break it,' Simon urged.

She looked up at him drily, shaking her head.

He touched her cheek as he had once before, his finger light and cool against her skin. 'Will it do any harm to have dinner with me? I won't insist you ask me in afterwards.'

'I don't break dates,' said Laura, aware that her nerves were jangling as his finger trailed down her cheek.

'Start now.'

She shook her head, smiling lightly.

'The next evening,' he suggested, raising one eyebrow in a dry, quizzical fashion as though expecting a second refusal.

Laura hesitated. Don't be stupid, her mind told her. Only a crazy fool would risk seeing him again. She listened to that quiet internal voice and then said: 'All right, thank you.'

You idiot, she thought, mentally kicking herself. Why did you say that?

'I'll pick you up at seven,' he said, smiling with obvious surprise. Turning away, he opened the door and Laura walked after him, still scolding herself.

'Goodnight,' he told her as he went, a thread of open satisfaction in his voice. 'See you!'

Laura closed the front door and leaned on it. Was there a streak of suicidal insanity in the Sloane family after all? Her mind had given her all the warnings she could need. What had made her say yes after that? Face burning, she refused to admit to herself what answer came to that question. She told herself, instead, that if she kept Simon's attention fixed on her he wouldn't be chasing Annette over the next weeks. It was a good enough reason, wasn't it? If one were looking for an excuse that would do.

And I'm looking for an excuse, she thought wryly. Despite all the cool reasoning of her brain, she had been torn apart when he stood there waiting for her answer, his finger smoothing down her cheek. When instinct and emotion fought against reason, did they have to win every time? Surely she could listen to her mind and not her body once in a while?

In the past there had never been any conflict. Her mind had always won because her body hadn't offered any contest. No man had ever made her feel the way Simon Hilliard did.

Was it purely sexual response? That hadn't occurred to her until now. He made her heart beat faster, made her blood sing in her ears, but was it a physical reaction or were her emotions actually involved at last?

Laura refused to think about that. She switched off the lights and made her way to bed thinking resolutely about her book. Her work was a safe subject which had never failed before. Tonight it was having difficulty engaging her attention, but she was determined to make it occupy her mind. Somehow she was going to force the image of Simon Hilliard out of her distracted brain.

CHAPTER SEVEN

WHEN Simon picked her up the night of their date Laura was in full possession of all her faculties, having spent the intervening period in lecturing herself on the folly of losing her cool again. Simon's narrowed eyes flicked over her, reading her mood, she suspected from the hard smile he gave her as he looked back at her face.

'You look charming,' he flattered, and she smiled at him in mock gratitude.

'Thank you.' She had spent a long time in achieving the right look. Her cream dress was classical in style, the bodice high and accentuating her slender figure, the neckline modestly scooped so that the black ribbon round her neck gave the whole dress a Regency look. She wore a cameo pinned on the ribbon, but wished she hadn't when Simon bent deliberately to look at it far too closely.

'Nice,' he said, his head next to hers.

As he straightened his eyes were on her mouth, and Laura had to resist a temptation to move away. She wanted him to believe she was totally in control.

Well, I am, she told herself furiously, wishing she believed herself.

'I can almost see it,' Simon observed.

'What?' she asked, following him out to his car, her long skirts brushing the pavement.

'The "don't touch" sign.'

He opened the passenger door and she climbed into the car without answering, pretending to smile.

He had picked out a London restaurant which had a sweeping view of the river and the lights of the city across the other side. Dark blocks of office buildings edged the skyline like jagged teeth. The Thames had an oily black gleam which rippled here and there as a passing car hit it with its headlights.

Laura sipped her wine, staring out of the window. A fringed red lamp glowed on the table and gave them an illusion of privacy which the occasional voices around them disturbed.

Simon talked about a film he had just seen, advising her to see it. 'Have you seen the new Woody Allen film?'

She glanced round, her blonde hair swinging against her cheek. 'No, is it good?'

'Do you like him?'

'Yes.'

'It's good.' He grinned at her. 'You're either for or against with him, haven't you noticed? He's one of those subjects people can argue about for hours.'

'Annette can't stand him,' Laura agreed. 'She never sees the joke.'

'No,' he drawled, 'I can believe it.' Their eyes met and they both laughed.

'She hasn't much sense of humour,' Simon agreed. 'Now she's a typical Sloane.'

'I wish you'd stop talking about my family as though they were some sort of separate tribe!'

'You are,' he said, then leaned forward to refill her glass. 'Sorry, let's change the subject.'

The wine waiter appeared looking reproachful as though Simon had insulted him by pouring the wine himself. He took the bottle from him and coldly replaced it in the ice bucket before dematerialising again. Laura and Simon grinned at each other.

'Demarcation lines,' said Simon.

'I'm afraid so. You're threatening his job.'

He looked at her plate. 'Didn't you like the sole?'

'Very nice. I'm not hungry.'

'Neither am I,' he admitted drily. 'We must be in love.'

Laura gave him a cool stare. 'Not me,' she said.

'Of course, I'd forgotten. You're a Sloane.'

'Will you stop that?' Her eyes flared with impatience. 'I'm getting a bit sick of the joke!'

He grimaced. 'I keep trying to convince myself you're a Sloane, that's the trouble. Every time I look at you I find it harder and harder to believe. Are you sure your mother didn't short-change your father?'

'I beg your pardon?' Laura glared at him. 'That wasn't funny.'

Her tone made his brows rise. 'Sorry. Did I tread on some toes?'

'Did you ever meet my mother?' Laura had difficulty making herself speak normally. The only member of her family whom she had ever loved had been her mother. Laura had bitterly resented the way in which George Sloane had frozen his wife out of existence by sheer ruthless indifference.

Simon stared at her intently. 'No. What was she like? I've often wondered what sort of woman could bring herself to marry your father.'

'She wasn't easy to know,' Laura said huskily. 'She rarely said a word. She was gentle and quiet and very vulnerable.'

'And she was married to George Sloane? Poor woman.' Simon wasn't speaking lightly, his face dark.

'Yes,' said Laura, looking at her wine glass and

twisting it between cold fingers. She had often wondered what her mother thought about, but Meriel Sloane had not been given to confidences. Any pain she suffered had been shut inside her own head. She had drifted around the Sloane house like a gentle ghost until she died. Laura's sharpest memories of her had been those of early childhood, and their power had intensified as she got old enough to realise just how her father had drained all the life out of her mother over the years. She could remember enough of Meriel Sloane at an earlier age to know the difference between the silent, drawn woman of her adolescence and the mother she had known as a small girl.

Or was it merely that her mother had found it easier to give her affection freely towards a small child, secure in the knowledge that children always give back what is offered to them? A child turns instinctively to the warmth of a smile, a word of affection. It is far harder to offer love to a teenager or an adult. One never knows if it is wanted or will be given back. A child will run to throw its arms around its parent without thinking or becoming selfconscious, but during the years of adolescence the giving of love becomes fraught with awareness and a fear of looking foolish. Remembering her own teenage years, Laura hoped she hadn't increased her mother's isolation by becoming too prickly and difficult, but she knew she had hung back when she might have shown her mother far more often what she felt. The insecurity of teenage feelings always seems to raise barriers even when the love of a parent is present. Growing up in a house where open expression of affection was almost non-existent, Laura had turned in upon herself even more than other teenagers.

'I've heard about her,' said Simon, and Laura was shaken out of her unhappy memories to look at him.

'Who from? People in the firm? They barely knew her.'

'You were very fond of her?'

'Yes,' said Laura, bending her head. The pressure of all the things she did not say lay heavily on her mind. She had never discussed her mother with anyone. She did not even know what Philip or Annette thought of the relationship between their parents. The Sloanes were not a family given to such discussion. Annette talked enough, God knew, but she was only interested in herself and her own concerns. She had little time to spare for anyone else.

'And your father? Are you fond of him?' Simon's drawl was sardonic and Laura met his eyes with a cool little smile.

'I'm not discussing my father with you!'

'He's a sore subject,' he agreed. The waiter appeared and began to remove their barely touched plates, looking at them in offended surprise.

'Was something wrong with the sole, sir?'

'No, we aren't hungry,' Simon apologised, and the man gave him a pitying look as though they had to be lunatics if they were prepared to order and then pay for food they had not touched.

'Coffee?' Simon asked Laura.

'Please,' she said and the waiter hovered, asking: 'No sweet, madam?'

'No, just coffee,' she said, and with a faint sniff he vanished to get the coffee.

Laura looked at her fingers, plaiting them on the table, the pearly shimmer of her nails given a pink tinge by the table lamp. 'What has my father done to you?' she asked.

'To me?' He leaned back, his wide shoulders level and stiff. 'Not much. He paid me personally very well.'

'You know what I mean. What have you got against him?'

'Aside from the fact that he skimps on safety measures in the factories, questions every penny that's spent, is acid and unpleasant in argument, and never forgets a grievance, you mean?'

Laura met his green eyes. 'Yes. That doesn't explain the very personal feeling you have against him.'

'Doesn't it?' He was mocking her again, his mouth wry.

'Black, madam?' The waiter appeared with the coffee and Simon watched as he added cream to Laura's cup before moving over to offer some to Simon.

When he had gone, Laura watched the pale rings of cream sinking into her coffee. 'I'm not stupid.'

'I didn't think you were,' he told her before she could go on. 'On the contrary, I'd say you were very shrewd. Your intelligence is obvious.'

'Thank you.' Her voice snapped slightly. She had the feeling he wasn't being flattering.

'I wasn't being sarcastic.'

She looked up from her contemplation of the coffee and he looked at her with dry appraisal. 'You're touchy on the subject, aren't you? Why should you want to hide your intelligence?'

Laura made a little face. 'I suppose most men find it unattractive. I'm always being told I'm intelligent, but always in a voice which conveys that the man resents it.'

'You must know a lot of men with inferiority complexes.'

She laughed. 'That must be it. Why didn't that occur to me?'

'I shouldn't think there was much else about you they objected to,' he drawled, his glance sliding down over her in silent comment.

Her colour rose. 'My sense of humour seems to bother them.'

Simon's brows shot up. 'Maybe you exercise it at the wrong moments. I did notice a tendency that way the other night.'

Laura's mouth curved in amusement. 'Sorry.'

'Although that was less a sign of humour than a deliberate taking down of the temperature, wasn't it?'

'Was it?' Laura met his eyes without a flicker of reaction. He opened his mouth to answer and she was suddenly filled with a sort of panic. 'But we're getting off the point,' she said before he could say whatever he had been about to say.

He gazed at her unreadably. 'Which was? I've forgotten.'

'My father,' she said tartly, not believing him for a second.

'Not my favourite topic of conversation. Shall we forget him? He could spoil an otherwise very enjoyable evening.' He picked up his cup and sipped his coffee. 'Would you like a liqueur with this, by the way?'

'No, thank you,' said Laura, realising that he meant what he said and was not going to reopen the subject of her father.

'Were you good at art at school?' he asked, taking them right away from the subject.

'Not bad,' she said. 'What about you? What were you good at?'

His eyes teased. 'Collecting girlfriends. It was my only hobby.'

'I'm sure,' she said drily. 'Not electronics, then?'

'I fiddled around with radio parts. We had a ham radio enthusiast as a science master, and he taught me quite a bit about circuit building. He and I built a TV set together for the school.'

'Did it work?'

'Did it work?' he repeated, laughing. 'Of course it worked. What a question! You've insulted me now.' He looked round for the waiter and got the bill.

On the drive back to her flat, Laura began to get surges of panic running through her. Simon wasn't talking at all, which made it worse. She didn't know what he was thinking about, but she had a sinking suspicion his thoughts were running in the same general direction as her own. The car seemed claustrophobic, far too small, shutting them in together with the windy night outside and very far away.

He parked outside her flat and turned, his arm moving along the seat. Laura was sitting tensely in her seat, wondering whether to leap out of the car, as her instinct suggested, or brave it out with a bright little smile as though her body wasn't quivering with nervous expectation.

Simon's amused glance didn't help. 'Thank you for a very pleasant evening,' he said softly, with a formality which didn't lessen her tension in the least. She did not believe in it. She felt like someone confronting a couched tiger and knowing that any moment it was going to spring without knowing when.

'I enjoyed the meal very much,' she said.

'Even though you weren't hungry,' he murmured with a wicked, teasing smile.

'The coffee was very good,' Laura said, and he laughed.

She let a brief pause go by before she said: 'Well, thank you, anyway,' turning at the same moment to find the door handle.

'Laura,' Simon said softly at her back.

She tensed, still fiddling with the handle. 'Yes?'

He took hold of her shoulder and turned her without undue pressure or haste so that she faced him. 'Haven't you forgotten something?'

She stared helplessly at his mouth, following the hard certain curve of it with absorption. 'What?' she asked huskily, feeling her breathing quicken in a way which was becoming all too familiar.

'Your handbag,' he said, picking it up from the floor and thrusting it into her hands.

Laura looked at it blankly and then looked at him. He was totally straightfaced, but his green eyes were gleaming with silent amusement.

She said, 'Thank you,' in the voice of someone longing to do something violent, and got herself out of the car before she did just that.

She walked off, hearing the exhaust roar as he drove away, and let herself into her flat. She was in no state to go to bed and sleep. She put on a record and made herself some cocoa, crouching on the rug in front of the electric fire and listening to a smoky whispering song which so exactly suited her mood that she played it again when it had ended.

What on earth is the matter with me? she asked herself angrily. Anyone would think I resented the fact that he didn't kiss me. I was terrified he would and when he didn't I felt as if he'd laughed in my face. Am I going out of my mind?

It was insane to feel frustrated and on edge because something you had been dreading hadn't happened.

She had the awful feeling that Simon had calculated her reaction exactly. His eyes had been wicked with amusement as she snatched her bag from him.

Finishing her cocoa, she switched off both fire and record player and stamped off to bed, scolding herself all the way.

When she got up in the morning she was in a very different mood. She hadn't slept well and when she did sleep had been troubled with dreams she preferred to forget in the morning. Irritable, tense, she forced all thought of Simon out of her head and started work with determination.

Declan had sent her the text of the children's book he wanted her to illustrate. She hadn't yet had time to read it, but that evening, tired after a long struggle to concentrate when her head ached and her eyes were sandy from lack of sleep, she sat down with the manuscript and began to read it while she ate a sandwich.

She was laughing within two pages. By the time she had finished it she knew she wanted badly to illustrate it. The characters were all animals and birds with bizarre human characteristics and the storyline was at one and the same time absurd and entirely realistic. Things happened with haphazard abruptness yet were always strictly practical.

Laura was so excited she rang Declan, which was a mistake, since he was so delighted to hear that she was going to accept that he talked for ages about later books which the author planned. Laura got a distinct feeling that he intended her to work on them too and that her own writing would be a thing of the past if Declan had his way.

'About money,' she said at last, when she was unable to stop him any other way.

'Yes,' he said enthusiastically. 'I'm absolutely delighted that you're going to do the book. See you on Tuesday at lunch.'

He was gone like bathwater going down the drain. Laura laughed as she put down the phone. It never failed!

Her smile went as she contemplated the idea of becoming a full-time illustrator for someone else's books. She looked at the manuscript. She had to recognise that this man was exceptional. In its odd way the book was almost a work of genius, strongly individual and hilariously funny. She knew perfectly well that she would never be able to write anything half as good. That was why Declan had switched her to doing factual books. Her artwork was far better than her text and she was sufficiently honest to admit it to herself. She wasn't original enough.

She was looking forward to meeting the author. She had gained a picture of him from the book itself and she wondered how far his own looks and personality would match his writing.

On the day of their lunch she felt quite excited as she went to meet Declan and the unknown author of *Bat Holiday*.

For once Declan was punctual. He arrived a moment after Laura, charging across the restaurant, dragging someone behind him like a trophy seized in battle.

Laura shook hands with the tiny thin man who emerged from behind Declan, wondering if it was true

that the fantastic adventures in the book had been
spawned inside so small and ordinary-looking a head.

He was incredibly neat—tiny hands and feet, a pale
nervous face, hair well brushed and very conventional
clothes. At first sight he might have been a clerk or a
salesman who rarely sold anything. He did not look like
a man capable of making anyone howl with laughter.

'Henry has indigestion, I'm afraid,' Declan told her
as they were studying the menu in silence only broken
by Declan at intervals.

Henry blushed and ducked down his head, as though
aghast to hear Declan admit it to her.

'Oh, dear,' Laura said helplessly.

'He can only eat boiled fish,' Declan declared.

Henry squirmed and made protesting noises.

Laura looked at the menu. 'There doesn't seem to
be any boiled fish here,' she pointed out.

The waiter hovered, staring at Henry, whose ears
had turned scarlet. 'Is there any boiled fish?' Declan
asked. 'My friend can only eat boiled fish.'

'No!' Henry gasped, and pointed at the menu with a
shaking finger. The waiter looked over his shoulder.

'Omelette, sir?'

Henry nodded and subsided into silence while
Declan and Laura gave their orders. When the waiter
had gone, Declan kindly asked Henry if he was sure an
omelette would be safe.

'Yes,' Henry whispered.

'Because if you want to change your mind we can
always get them to boil you some fish,' Declan urged.

'No,' said Henry.

Laura caught his eye. She was certain he was laughing, but his face stayed completely blank.

During the meal it was Declan who did all the talking. Henry sat and listened and looked at the table-cloth. Once or twice he arranged the cutlery in a new pattern or adjusted his tie, otherwise he might have been a statue.

Declan saw a friend on the other side of the restaurant while they were having coffee. Excusing himself, he dashed over to say a few words and Laura searched her mind for something to say to the silent little figure opposite her.

Without raising his eyes Henry suddenly murmured: 'He's like a puppy whose feet are too big.'

Laura looked at him in wild surmise. 'A puppy?'

'And a voice that's louder than you think.'

'Declan?' Laura glanced across at where he was talking with those sweeping, energetic gestures. 'He's a bit big for a puppy.'

'That's why his feet are too big,' Henry said. 'He trips over them.'

Laura looked back at him. 'Do you always see people as animals?'

Henry glanced up shyly. 'Yes.'

'Your book——' Laura began, and Henry smiled. 'Yes.'

'All people?'

'Yes.'

'Good Lord!' Laura exclaimed. 'That frog . . .'

'My mother-in-law.'

Laughing, she asked: 'And the bat?'

Henry didn't answer, ducking his head again.

On a sudden inspiration Laura said: 'You?' then hoped she hadn't offended him.

'Yes,' said Henry with a quiet pride that made her laugh again. 'Does it help?' he asked.

Laura stared for a moment before she saw what he

meant. 'For the artwork? Oh, yes, enormously. I should have seen it at once. I thought they had strong human characteristics.'

Henry coughed. 'Would you mind if . . .' He broke off and gave her another surreptitious look from under his eyelashes. 'I would like to see some of your work.'

'Before we come to a final decision?' She could see that she was going to have to work hard in conversation with Henry. He tended to leave all the t's uncrossed and expect you to cross them for him.

'I'm sure you're very . . .'

'All the same, you want to be certain,' she agreed.

'If you don't . . .' Henry gave her a helpless, appealing smile.

'Of course not. How would it be if I did some little sketches of the bat for a start?'

'Batty,' he said in a tender voice. 'Declan wanted to change the name.'

'Oh, no,' said Laura, 'it suits him,' then wondered again if she had said the right thing in view of the fact that the bat was Henry himself in another form.

Apparently she had, for Henry looked shyly pleased. His neat little hands made elegant passes over the tablecloth as though he were about to conjure up a bat from the sugar bowl.

'I'm glad.'

'Shall I send you the sketches?'

'Please,' he said. 'Declan does rather . . .' He tailed off again, leaving that in the air.

'Rush you into things?' Laura enquired.

He looked at her gratefully.

Laura smiled. 'Don't worry. I've got a feeling we can work together.'

'Yes,' Henry agreed, nodding.

She considered him for a moment. After a hesitation she asked: 'How do you see me? What am I?'

'A mongoose,' he said, confounding her.

She had half expected him to name some elegant animal like a gazelle. Laughter broke out of her, her blue eyes dancing with amusement.

'Small and deadly,' Henry said, adding soberly, 'especially if you're a snake.'

'Thank you,' Laura drawled, not quite sure whether to be flattered or horrified by the comparison.

Declan rushed back to them, exclaiming with apologies, and a short time later they parted. When she was back at her flat Laura thought back over what Henry had said about her, rather appalled in retrospect. A mongoose? Small and deadly?

Thinking of snakes made her mind move to Simon. She would have a chance to discuss him with her brother that evening over dinner, she realised. Philip was easier to corner than either her father or Simon. She might get something out of him, although if George Sloane had buried his secret as well as he usually did it was unlikely that Philip knew anything. And if he did, he might be too scared to talk.

Laura had rung her father that morning to tell him she was having Philip and Daphne to dinner and invite him to join them. He had been reluctant to talk on the phone, his voice brusque. 'Sorry, too busy. Thanks for asking. Have a good dinner.'

'Are you all right, Father?' she had asked tentatively, and he had said in a sharp voice: 'Of course I am. Don't fuss!' Then he had hung up and she had grimaced at the phone before she replaced it. It was a waste of time expecting his approaching operation to have any effect on his stoic and inhuman character.

The threat of death wasn't softening him. She wondered if he even thought about it as he went on with his work. Surely even her father must pause to consider death? Or did he just push it aside as irrelevant and get on with what had to be dealt with at that moment?

She could not remember anything piercing the stone shell of his nature. Looking back over her years at home she could not recall one instant when she had seen his feelings revealed. Did he have any? Her mother's death had passed over him as though it had nothing to do with him at all. Laura had grieved in private and made no attempt to offer him comfort because she had seen no break in his cold manner. The only feelings he ever showed were irritation and terse impatience.

She had prepared most of the dinner in advance, planning cold dishes chiefly, with a main course of salmon steaks in a bland sauce which could be kept hot without spoiling. Daphne and Philip would be punctual; it was a religion with them.

They arrived exactly on time. Daphne was carrying a large box of very expensive gilt-wrapped mints and Philip held a bottle of wine. They presented them to her with bright smiles and both accepted a glass of sherry.

'What a nice flat you've got,' Daphne congratulated her, glancing around as she held her glass with something of reproof, as though the sherry disagreed with her. Her eye was caught by a picture. Laura saw her stare. 'That's an interesting painting. One of yours?'

'Salvador Dali, actually,' said Laura, glancing at the surrealist landscape.

Philip was gazing at it, dumbfounded. 'That watch is melting,' he said.

'Yes,' Laura agreed.

'Why is it?' he asked.

'God knows. I hope you both like salmon.'

'Oh, yes,' said Daphne, 'we do.'

'Salmon—lovely!' Philip said brightly. 'We never have it at home.'

Daphne glared at him. 'Yes, we do. Often.'

'Sometimes,' he temporised.

They both beamed at Laura, as though daring her to notice that they had come close to a quarrel. She wondered if their idyllic marriage were quite so idyllic after all.

'Can I help?' Daphne asked, making little gestures with her untouched glass.

'Don't you like sherry?' Laura asked.

'Yes, of course,' said Daphne.

Philip opened his mouth to say something, then caught Daphne's eye and shut it again. Daphne drank her sherry with a suppressed shudder.

'Philip can give me a hand carrying things in,' said Laura, moving towards the kitchen.

Daphne went over to stare disapprovingly at the Salvador Dali, while Philip followed his sister into the kitchen and helplessly gazed around him. 'What can I do?'

'How are things at the firm?' Laura asked, getting out the table mats.

'Fine,' Philip said enthusiastically.

'Father O.K.?'

'Fine,' said Philip with less enthusiasm.

'And how are you and Daphne?'

'Fine,' Philip said again with the faintest touch of

gloom. He laughed nervously. 'Off and on. You know how it is—marriage and all that.'

'I know how it is,' Laura agreed. 'I got the idea from Father that things were a bit tough in the firm.'

'A bit,' Philip said cautiously, looking at her as though trying to guess how much she knew.

'Father's worried about Simon Hilliard,' Laura said very casually.

Philip's face changed. 'Yes,' he said, a spot of red in each cheek.

Surprised, she asked: 'Are you?'

He gave her a hunted, alarmed look. He glanced at the door and went over to shut it, to her amazement. Lowering his voice, he said: 'Not so loud. Daphne might hear us.'

'She doesn't know?' Laura asked, wondering what on earth it was that Daphne didn't know and why it was so important that she shouldn't know.

'Good Lord,' exclaimed Philip, his redness growing, 'of course not!'

'No, of course not,' Laura agreed slowly, thinking hard. 'You wouldn't want her to find out.' Find out what? she thought.

'Last person in the world,' said Philip, his head bent.

'She wouldn't like it,' Laura said, wondering how on earth to tackle the question without revealing how little she herself knew.

'Never forgive me,' Philip muttered, shuffling his feet. 'I mean, before I met her and all that, but all the same. No point in confessions, I always think.'

'Simon Hilliard wouldn't tell her?' Laura asked, drawing a bow at a tangent.

Philip's head shot up and a horrified look dawned

on his face. 'He isn't threatening to? Father didn't tell
me that. Good God, that's blackmail! Hilliard's a
tough egg, but surely he wouldn't do a rotten thing
like that? I mean, all water under the bridge, over
years ago. Okay, I didn't show up too well, but if he'd
meant to drop me in it he would have done it years
ago.' He paused, thinking. 'No, he wouldn't. I don't
mind Hilliard myself. Father detests him. Hilliard
blamed him, not me, you know—told me so. A bit
rude, actually, said I was a spineless jelly.' He laughed
uncomfortably. 'A bit of truth in that, I suppose. But I
can't believe Hilliard would talk to Daphne. What
made you think he might?'

'I just wondered,' said Laura, trying to sort out all
that he had said and make some definite pattern out of
it.

'No, no,' Philip assured her, 'he wouldn't. Of
course, he's got his eyes on the business. Well, he
knows too much. Knows where all the bodies are
buried, see what I mean?'

'I see what you mean,' Laura agreed.

'Father should never have quarrelled with him, but
after I married Daphne the balloon went up. Hilliard
was spoiling for a fight after that. He's damned clever,
you know—got me beaten into a cocked hat.'

Laura looked at him with amusement. 'That's very
honest of you, Philip.'

He looked at her glumly. 'I'll never manage to run
the firm, you know. Too much damned hard work.
It's killing Father.'

'I hope not,' said Laura, her smile vanishing.

'Anything wrong?' Daphne had pushed open the
door and was staring at them in faintly accusing fashion.

'Sorry, we got talking,' Laura apologised. 'Can you

take these in, Philip? We're ready now, Daphne.'

It was the last chance she had to speak to her brother alone, but she felt she had learned enough, anyway. Whatever Philip had been talking about it was clear that Simon's grievance against her father was entirely personal and to do with something Philip had done in the past. Laura's mind boggled as she tried to imagine her meek, ineffectual brother doing anything in the slightest degree reprehensible. But obviously Philip had done something. What?

CHAPTER EIGHT

HER father moved into the hospital days before his operation. Laura wouldn't have known anything about it if she hadn't rung him by sheer accident and had him brusquely inform her that he was going into hospital the following morning. 'I have to be prepared for the operation for some time, it seems. They want to run various tests and make sure I'm in a safe condition to have it.'

'Shall I be able to visit you?' Laura asked.

'No need,' he said in a curt voice.

'Father, I'd like to!'

'They want me to rest,' he said, and she realised that he didn't want her to visit him. There was no point in arguing; George Sloane was immovable when he had made up his mind.

'Which hospital, anyway?' she asked. 'I'd like to send you some flowers.'

'Can't stand them.'

'All the same, won't you tell me which hospital?' She tried to sound coaxing, her voice carrying a smile, although his obstinacy was making her both angry and sad.

He told her reluctantly. 'My secretary will give you any news you should have,' he added.

A daily bulletin sent out by telex? Laura thought. All very neat and impersonal but businesslike, of course.

'Good luck,' she told her father, trying to sound calm and confident that everything was going to go well. 'After the operation, can I visit you, please?'

'If they let you,' he said, and rang off with a muttered word. Laura put the phone down, sighing, and tried to concentrate on her work. Her mind was divided. How was she supposed to work with a head full of anxieties about her father, Annette, Simon's intentions? People were a constant source of anxiety. When she had finished work for the day she could put away her brushes, her paints, shut her workroom door on them all and forget work for a while. But people won't be shut up into a tidy box. They push their way into your head and refuse to be evicted, however hard you try to get rid of them.

Her book was almost finished now; she only had a few more drawings to do. She was already beginning to think more about Henry's book than her own. He had approved the bat sketches she had done and it was now definite that she would be illustrating his book. Declan was delighted that they got on. 'I knew you would,' he had boasted. 'You've both got a great sense of humour.'

'We need one, with you,' Laura had told him. 'About money . . .'

'We'll discuss that next time,' Declan had told her hurriedly, ringing off before she could insist on a discussion right then.

The more Laura thought about Henry's book, the more she looked forward to working on it. In his own way, Declan was a genius, she decided. He worked on instinct and in this case the instinct had been dead right. He had guessed that Laura and Henry would make a matching pair and Laura had to admit she was grateful to him. She had no intention of telling him so, however. Declan already believed himself to be a genius; she wasn't going to encourage him to become even more conceited.

She caught herself drawing little bats everywhere, in the margins of magazines, on the backs of envelopes, all of them with Henry's neat little fingers and secretly humorous eyes.

On the following Saturday morning she met Donald while she was doing her shopping in Hampstead Village. He was standing in front of a chemist's with an abstracted expression, in danger of being run over by a pram being wheeled right at him by a girl in jeans and a ferocious expression. Laura yanked him out of her path and the girl sailed past with the air of one who would dearly have loved to run him over.

Startled, Donald said: 'Oh, hallo, I didn't see you there.' He seemed to have missed the entire incident of the pram from the way he was looking at Laura in reproach. 'Sorry,' he added, being Donald and very well brought up.

Laura smiled at him. 'Forgotten something?'

He touched his jacket pocket vaguely. 'I had a list, but I seem to have mislaid it. My mother wanted something from the chemist. I got the frozen prawns, but I can't remember what else she wanted.'

'You could ring and ask her,' Laura suggested.

'She's in bed with migraine,' said Donald, his comic face rather pink. 'She hasn't been too well lately.'

Since she heard he had got engaged to Annette? thought Laura.

'How's Annette?' she asked, and Donald looked melancholy.

'Fine.' He didn't sound too sure, nor did he look the

picture of a happily engaged man.

'Have you fixed a wedding date yet?'

'Annette thought next spring,' he told her. 'You have to book up months in advance, it seems. There are lots of arrangements to be made, it can't be done in a hurry.' She got the feeling he was repeating what Annette had told him—or were these his mother's words?

'She's planning a mammoth wedding?' Laura could believe it. Annette would enjoy being the star of a big show. No hole-and-corner weddings for her. She would sweep down the aisle in lace and silk to the silver sounds of 'Oh, for the wings ...' and enjoy every second of it, including the packed reception with the cold buffet and table groaning under the weight of wedding presents. The picture made Laura shudder. If she ever married she would elope, she decided.

'She wants a big wedding,' Donald admitted gloomily. 'Top hat and morning suit.' She saw that to him this was the real horror. He did not look forward to being stared at in formal gear, dressed up like a performing elephant. He had all the normal male dislike of appearing in public in fancy dress, but Laura didn't need three guesses as to who would win the battle of the wedding arrangements. Annette would have an easy victory. That, no doubt, was why Donald's mother had gone to bed with migraine, retiring from the field of battle. Poor Donald, no wonder he looked hagridden!

'Well, so long as you're both happy,' she said brightly, and Donald tried to look rapturous without much success.

'Annette's on top of the world,' he did confide. 'We're having an engagement party when your father gets back from the States.'

Laura just about managed to look as if she wasn't taken aback. So that was what their father had told Annette!

'Don't forget to invite me,' she told him.

'Oh, we wouldn't,' he said, shocked.

'What present shall I get? What's Annette hoping for?'

Donald looked at the sky for inspiration. 'She's got lists,' he said, leaving Laura with a picture of Annette with sheafs of paper making out huge lists of things she could not start married life without.

'I'll give her a ring and ask her,' she told him.

'That's a good idea,' he said, relieved. 'I don't know. She seems to want so many things.'

He was beginning to know Annette, Laura thought, as she left him and walked away. Was his first ecstatic delight wearing off? The life of a married man might not seem so fabulous to him when he found himself engulfed in wedding present lists and quarrels over guests between his mother and Annette.

At least while Annette was so absorbed in all that she was unlikely to be secretly dating Simon Hilliard at the same time. Laura told herself that her relief about that was entirely due to a sisterly concern for Annette and a desire to protect her father. It had nothing whatever to do with Simon Hilliard himself.

She hadn't heard from him since the night they had dinner together. She told herself she was glad about that, but every time the phone rang or someone came to the front door, she found her heart racing as she rushed to answer. It was never Simon, and the sickening plunge with which she faced that made her increasingly angry with herself.

He was becoming a fixation. She spent far too much time thinking about him. Her sense of humour had so far failed to laugh her out of it and her cool common sense seemed unable to deal with the emotions she was struggling against. Whenever she found him inside her head she tried to think of something else, but he was insidious; he kept on coming back. If Laura relaxed her guard for a second she would start remembering things she didn't want to remember.

It was crazy to feel like this about him when she knew he had strong reasons for hating her family. When her father first mentioned him and accused him of trying to seduce Annette as some sort of revenge against the Sloanes, Laura had thought it an absurd suspicion. She had not been able to believe that anyone could behave like that—except possibly her own father. What she had learnt of Simon since had made her change her mind. Charming and amusing though he was, he had an undeniable obsession about her family and he hadn't hidden his desire to hit back at her father by any means he could find.

I wish I knew what was behind it all, Laura thought, as she did one of the last drawings for her book. The sky was a cool pale blue, the sun watery. She lifted her head to look out of the window, wishing she could keep her mind on her work long enough to finish the book. It was the first time she had ever had difficulty concentrating on a book.

She had always prided herself on her ability to concentrate, to ignore anything which might disrupt her working mood, but in a few short weeks Simon had wrecked her whole scheme of living. Watching other people in love, Laura had often thought that they were to be pitied, their minds clouded by illusion which would wear off all too soon. She had been grateful for having escaped that sort of lunacy, confident that her rational attitude to life would protect her from their folly.

She was beginning to be afraid she had been wrong. She wasn't yet prepared to put the name love to how she felt about Simon; she wasn't sure what to call it. But it was powerful, and however hard she struggled she seemed to get deeper into it with every day.

Every time she remembered her own feelings while he was kissing her she felt oddly fevered, her limbs weak and trembling. That sort of excitement was a drug to which she could become addicted, and the only way to avoid addiction was to avoid Simon.

If he tried to see her again, she told herself, she would refuse firmly. He wasn't trapping her in that sort of situation.

Yet when the phone rang she snatched it up, her stomach tightening. 'Yes?' She was so nervous she was barely able to speak, her voice breathless.

'Have dinner with me?'

The drawled voice made her heart stop and begin again with a terrifying urgency.

All her plans for treating him with cool indifference vanished from her head. It didn't even occur to her to pretend she did not know who it was.

'Oh,' she stammered, her skin suddenly burning. She put a hand to her face and almost snatched it away at the heat she could feel.

'Yes or no?' he asked almost aggressively.

'When?' she asked, abandoning all thought of a refusal without a second's hesitation.

'Tonight.'

'Tonight,' Laura murmured, still struggling between sanity and the desire to see him again.

'Yes or no?' he asked again, his tone harsh.

'Yes,' she said before she could change her mind, as though she was afraid of the very sanity which was the only thing which could save her from such idiocy.

'I'll pick you up at eight,' he said. 'I've got a heavy day today and I'll have to work late.'

She began to say something, but he had hung up abruptly. Laura put the phone down and began cursing herself. He hadn't sounded as though he particularly wanted to see her. She had almost felt there was hostility in his crisp voice. Why had he invited her if he was in that sort of mood? And why had she been stupid enough to accept?

That evening as she got ready she felt like someone on the edge of a volcano, aware that it might erupt at any moment, and that anyone with any sense would leave the district without a second's thought. She had spent the last few days telling herself over and over again not to see Simon, yet the moment he rang she had accepted a date almost without thinking. She was beginning to be scared of her own weakness.

Once she would have said with amused certainty that no man could talk her into bed if she was determined not to give way, but although she kept telling herself how idiotic it would be to let Simon within an inch of her, she had a sinking feeling that the moment he tried she would melt into helpless response.

She was melting now at the very idea of being in his arms, her body trembling. She looked at her flushed face in the mirror with impatience. Where's your self-control? she asked herself. Where's your sense of humour, for God's sake? You've laughed other men out of the door. Why can't you laugh at him? At yourself, even? If you saw this happening to someone else, you'd wonder if they were quite right in the head. Have you gone crazy, after all?

Perhaps that was what had happened, she thought. She had temporarily become insane. A mid-summer madness, she told herself. Was that what it was?

She should have sensed the danger the first time he kissed her. Why hadn't she started to run then, and kept on running?

Because she had refused to admit to herself that she was in any danger, she thought wryly. Her ego wouldn't let her admit that she could ever suffer the throes of an infatuation. But that was what was wrong with her. In the teeth of all sense she was being dragged into a hectic infatuation with a man she knew could be dangerous to her.

Even when he had not tried to kiss her on their last evening together she had not been relieved—merely frustrated. She couldn't tell herself Simon was trying to sweep her off her feet, which might have been some consolation. The danger wasn't Simon, it was herself.

She was ready far too early. It left too much time free for her to prowl around the flat like a restless animal in a cage, trying to stop herself thinking about Simon, trying to lecture herself on keeping calm. Her mind had run out of her control like a horse that has stampeded. She picked up ornaments and put them down, looked out of the window, turned on the radio and turned it off, knowing that her whole attention was given to waiting for Simon to arrive.

When the doorbell did go she jumped about ten feet in the air and felt her hands shaking as she walked out of the sitting-room. She was so furious with herself that she was frowning as she opened the door.

Simon's usual charming, mocking smile was absent. Laura looked at him with an assumed coolness, seeing his frown with an immediate frisson of impatience. He had said he was going to be having a heavy day, and clearly he had had one. He looked as on edge as she felt herself, but probably for very different reasons.

'Ready?' he asked without making any polite remarks about it being nice to see her.

'Yes,' said Laura, on the verge of snapping. If he was in a temper it would be better if they ditched the idea of having dinner, she thought, but she meekly closed the door and followed him out of the building.

'Have you been very busy?' she asked him. 'Was it a bad day?'

'Yes,' he muttered, opening the car and watching her get into it.

As he started the engine she stared at his hands on the wheel. There was suppressed impatience in their movements. He was physically on edge.

She wondered what was bothering him, and stole a furtive glance sideways at his face. The first time they met she remembered thinking that the strong structure of that face gave no clue to his nature at all. He had been laughing that night, amused satisfaction in his eyes as he talked to Annette. He wasn't laughing now. He was grim-faced, his mouth a straight hard line, his brows level and frowning above the green yes.

'Where are we dining?' she asked brightly.

His eyes flicked to her and away. 'Roland's, do you know it?'

'Vaguely.' She had heard the name but she couldn't recall ever having been there. 'Is it good food?'

'What?' He gave her another brief look. 'Oh, yes.'

My God, she thought, her teeth coming together, he might make an effort! If this was how he was going to be all evening they might as well call a halt right here and now.

As though he was trying to shake himself free of his mood, he asked: 'How's the book?'

'Fine,' she said, smiling far too cheerfully, her face stiff as it pulled with the movement of her mouth. She hoped he couldn't see how false her smile really was. 'I've almost finished it.'

'Then what?'

'Oh, I've been commissioned to do the artwork for someone else's book,' she told him with a sensation of relief at having a safe topic to talk about. She began to tell him about Henry and the bats. She wasn't sure he was really listening, although he smiled once or twice. But it kept the ball of conversation rolling and eliminated those nasty silences. If she was boring him, tough luck.

He interrupted her monologue suddenly to ask: 'Are you planning to marry this Declan?'

'Declan?' It was a few seconds before Laura remembered that she was supposed to be dating Declan and her blank tone must have been betraying, because Simon's green eyes narrowed on her, their expression hard and searching, and she hurriedly added: 'We haven't talked about it.'

'Not a very urgent relationship, then,' Simon said drily.

'We're both very busy,' Laura said airily before wondering if perhaps she might have phrased that better.

'Too busy to get married?' His brows arched.

'Well, you know how it is . . .' She knew she sounded fatuous and scrambled desperately to reach

some sort of safe ground before she got dangerously
bogged down in a discussion of Declan. 'I thought you
were going to Paris.' At once she wished she hadn't
mentioned Paris. It conjured up Annette.

'I've been,' he said. 'I've just got back.'

She felt sick relief. 'Oh. Did you enjoy yourself?'
No, she thought, wrong question, why did I ask him
that? Her face was burning.

He gave her a look from under his eyelashes. 'Now
how am I supposed to answer that?'

She prickled at the mockery in the tone. 'Don't
then,' she said, feeling like jumping out of the car.

'If I say I had a great time your imagination is going
to work overtime,' he drawled, 'and if I say I was
bored you're going to think I failed to click with
anyone.'

'I don't give a damn what you did,' Laura muttered,
staring out of the window. A black cat sat on the edge of
the curb as though waiting for the traffic to clear so that
it could cross. Laura stared at it fixedly. She refused to
think about what Simon had or hadn't done in Paris.

'I was working most of the time,' he said, and she
felt another sickening stab of relief. But then what
would he have said? He wasn't likely to tell her the
truth.

'It's none of my business what you got up to,' she
said, half to herself.

'No,' he said harshly, 'it isn't, so why the hell am I
explaining myself to you?'

'I didn't ask you to!'

They were almost snarling at each other, she realised, and both of them were staring straight ahead,
their bodies tense. The car was full of suppressed
anger.

What's the matter with him? she thought. Had he had a bad time in Paris? Was something wrong at his firm? There could be a dozen different reasons for his obvious ill temper, but she wished he wasn't taking it out on her.

He parked and they walked in a cold silence to the restaurant. Laura watched his black shadow leaping along the wall as they passed a street lamp. Her high heels clicked along the pavement, the echo bouncing back at her from the buildings on the other side of the street. She remembered telling herself that he had a sense of humour, but he hadn't got one tonight.

She had been sick with nerves about spending the evening with him. She had convinced herself that he was going to make a pass at her and she wasn't going to be able to resist him; now she was even wondering how she was going to get through the evening without hitting him over the head with a bottle of wine. If he kept up this terse, biting tone all evening she knew she was going to have no trouble at all in disliking him intensely.

The charm and humour she had come to expect were nowhere in sight. Simon ordered with scarcely a glance at her and then sat there with his eyes fixed on the table as though fascinated by the white damask cloth.

Laura looked around the crowded room. 'A full house,' she said lightly.

'Mm?' He looked up. 'Yes.'

'A popular spot, obviously,' she went on.

'Yes.' He resumed his study of the tablecloth.

Laura had the feeling that she would have to dance naked on the table to get his attention tonight. She

should be telling herself how relieved she was not to
be under the onslaught of those mocking green eyes.
She should be thanking God on her knees not to have
to struggle between common sense and a helpless attraction towards him. She did neither. She looked at
him bitterly and felt like kicking his ankle under the
table. At least it just might wake him out of his ab-
straction.

He had chosen fried whiting for his first course.
The tiny fish engaged all his attention, it seemed.
Laura fiddled with her melon, picking out small pieces
with meticulous care, trying to think of something to
say and failing.

They were both having coq au vin for the main
course. As the waiter moved away from the table,
having served them, Simon asked: 'Cat got your
tongue?'

The infamous question made her glare at him.
'Who, me?'

'You haven't said a thing for ten minutes.'

'I haven't noticed you falling over yourself to talk!'

He looked at his meal with distaste. 'I've got
something on my mind.'

'That's obvious.' She paused, then asked: 'What?'

He lifted his shoulders in an irritable shrug. 'It
doesn't matter.'

'Business?' Laura asked, giving him a second
chance.

He hesitated and gave her a brief, unreadable look.
'Not exactly.' There was a long pause during which
she thought of several biting things she would like to
say to him, then he asked: 'Where's your father?'

Laura stiffened. 'What?'

'He's supposed to be in the States,' Simon said,

prodding his chicken as though expecting it to bite him.

'Supposed to be? Isn't he?' Laura hedged.

'Not the way I heard it,' he said, giving her another quick sharp look.

Laura ate several tiny slivers of mushroom before she asked: 'What have you heard?'

'Rumours are hectic,' he explained. 'One story has it that he's on his way to a Swiss bank to grab his money and run. Another story says he's had a stroke.'

Laura sat upright, staring at him. 'They're both lies!' How had such stories started? Was her father's trust in his secretary misplaced? He had been so certain she was totally faithful. Had he been quite wrong about her?

'Where is he, though?' Simon enquired, still not looking at her. 'Don't tell me he's in the States. He isn't. Not in New York, anyway. I was talking to several people on the phone today, and he hasn't been over there lately.'

'Is that why you asked me out tonight? To pump me?' Laura was so angry her throat was raw. She pushed her plate away and sat very stiffly, glaring at him. 'Do you really expect me to give you details of what my father is doing?'

'The market's nervous about these rumours,' Simon told her curtly. 'Didn't you see the share prices today?'

'I'm not in the habit of studying them.'

'Philip hasn't told you that people are worried about your father's odd disappearance?'

'He hasn't disappeared!'

'Nobody seems to be sure where he is, though.'

'You keep your ear pretty close to the ground, don't

you? What has my father's whereabouts to do with
you?'

'If the firm is rocking I'm moving in to get it before
somebody else does,' Simon said tersely.

There was a silence. He looked up, a dark red spot
in each cheek. Laura looked at him directly, her blue
eyes icy.

'I see.'

'I've had long-term plans for taking it over for
years,' Simon told her almost belligerently. 'These
rumours started today. I don't know what began
them, but they were growing all day in the City and by
tomorrow share prices will be dropping unless your
father reappears and calms the whole storm down.' He
met her eyes with a dark frown. 'Will he do that?'

Laura swallowed the lump in her throat. 'You'll
have to wait and see, won't you?' She pushed back her
chair. 'Now, if you'll excuse me, I'll get a taxi to take
me home.'

'Don't be so damned stupid,' he snapped, rising to
snatch at her hand. 'I'll drive you.'

'No, thank you. Finish your dinner.'

'I don't want it,' he said.

The amused, curious stares of other diners were
fixed on them and Laura flushed as she realised how
much attention they were attracting.

'Sit down again,' Simon grated, refusing to let go of
her wrist. 'I'll get the bill.' He looked round impatiently, and their waiter appeared with a blank, polite
face. 'The bill, please,' Simon said, his tone daring the
man to comment.

Laura sat down, very flushed, and waited until
Simon had settled the bill. He guided her out of the
restaurant with a set expression on his face, ignoring

the looks which followed them.

In his car he sat with his hands on the wheel, his face in profile to her. 'Wouldn't it save a lot of trouble if you told me what was going on? By tomorrow morning I've got to make up my mind which way to jump.'

'That's entirely up to you,' shrugged Laura, hating him. This was precisely the situation her father had been afraid of when he refused to tell anyone the truth about his operation. She had thought he was being ridiculous, but now she saw George Sloane had judged the reaction very accurately. He knew the way the City would rush off in a panic if it suspected something was wrong. Laura had no idea whether her father would leave the hospital when he heard the rumours that were circulating, or whether his doctors would be able to insist that he go through with the operation in spite of his financial worries, but whichever way it was, she could see that this was going to be disastrous for his health. He wouldn't go into major surgery in any fit mental state if he was worrying about the firm. But if he left the operation until he had cleared all this up, he might leave it too late.

Simon stared at his hands, his black head bent. 'Laura,' he muttered huskily, 'try to understand.'

'Understand what? That you're trying to grab my father's firm?' she asked with a bitter smile.

'I'd laid my plans long ago,' Simon said in an edgy voice.

'My father was right about you, wasn't he? You're out for his blood—his and Philip's.'

His black head swung and she saw his face, pale and taut, his mouth a hard straight line. 'You know?' His voice was harsh.

Laura hesitated, on the point of pretending to know

more than she actually did know, then decided that that could be counter-productive and said: 'I know you hate them both. What did they do to you?'

For a long moment she thought he might actually tell her. His face was filled with doubt and struggle, then he said: 'Not me.'

'Who, then?' Laura asked, staring at him.

'I can't tell you. It isn't my story to tell. Ask your brother, if you really want to know.' He started the car, swinging away from her. The engine raced and then the car shot away from the curb, streaking through London's back streets like a bat out of hell. Simon brooded over the wheel, his brows frowning over his intent eyes.

'That's why you chased Annette, isn't it?' Laura asked him, staring at his averted profile. 'Revenge, that was all you wanted.'

'Not all,' he said with a sudden wry self-mockery. 'She's a very attractive specimen.'

'You make her sound like something in a jar!'

His mouth twisted. 'She is faintly subhuman. A typical Sloane.'

'Thank you!' Laura bit out, hating him again.

'You're a changeling,' Simon said roughly. 'I don't believe you're a Sloane at all. You must be a throw-back to some maternal ancestor.'

'Don't expect me to be grateful for that remark,' she snapped angrily.

'It was meant as a compliment.'

'Insulting my family is hardly a compliment to me!'

'Be honest are you crazy about them?' he asked drily, giving her a sideways smile. 'I suppose the best of the bunch is Philip, and he's a weak-kneed, spineless jellyfish.'

'Yet you were prepared to have an affair with An-nette,' Laura muttered, a jealous heat burning inside her.

He was silent, turning a corner at such high speed that the tires screeched and a man with a dog leapt on to the pavement in obvious terror of his life.

He pulled up outside her flat and sat facing the road, his black head sharply averted. 'I hadn't met you then,' he muttered.

Laura's heart nose-dived. She couldn't think of any thing to say. Did he mean it? Or was he still trying to weaken her resistance? The low harsh tone in which he had said it sounded sincere enough, but she could hardly be expected to trust a man whose declared intention was to take revenge on her whole family for some past action.

He shifted and she jumped, her breath stopping. Their eyes met in the shadows of the car, and she heard his breathing, fast and rough. Or was it her own she heard?

'Laura,' he whispered, moving forward. His hands framed her face. He stared at her mouth, the strong lines of his face fierce with an emotion she could feel yet not decipher. 'I can't make up my mind about you,' he said in that low, deep voice. 'It could all be illusion. Am I wrong about you?'

Before she could answer he was kissing her urgently, almost angrily, his mouth filled with hunger and passion, the pressure of it bruising her lips and making her very much aware of her own submerged need for the satisfaction she could feel he was demanding.

She forgot her anger, her distrust, her suspicion of him. Everything but desire was forced out of her and she melted into his arms, her body trembling, kissing him back heatedly with her arms around his bent head, caressing his hair and deeply aware of the modelling of his strong skull beneath her fingers. Under her passion she felt a flare of pain, as though she was afraid this was the last time she would ever see him.

Simon seemed to feel the same. A desperation held them together, like drowning swimmers, holding each other far too tight, their mouths meeting in a wild compulsion.

Breathing thickly, he buried his face in the side of her neck, his body shaking against hers. 'Let me come in. Laura, I need you. I'm going crazy. Let's forget everything else, just let me show you how I need you.'

She might have said yes. Every cell in her body was dissolving in the heat between them and her mind had stopped functioning on any level which could affect her decision. She was helpless in the grip of a burning desire for him which left no energy for anything but the satisfaction of its own impulse.

Some buried instinct held her silent for an instant. Her drowsy eyes stared out of the car, her lips parted to mutter 'Yes,' and another car shot past, headlights blazing into her. She blinked from the flash of orange light and shivered. The tiny incident broke up her fevered involvement with Simon, gave her mind a chance to work. It might be another attempt to revenge himself on one of the Sloanes. Carried away by her own feelings, how could she be sure of his? Was his urgent passion genuine? Or was he just trying to seduce her quite coldbloodedly?

He pulled back, looking at her harshly, his eyes all pupil and his face deeply flushed. 'Laura, for God's sake say yes-do you want to make me go out of my mind?'

She was hurriedly thinking back over his words. He hadn't mentioned love. He had talked of need, but not of love.

'I want you desperately,' he muttered, his hands biting into her shoulders as though to shake her into submission.

'No,' she said, dropping the word in a brittle coldness.

He froze, staring at her, anger burning in his eyes.

'Sorry,' Laura added with a false smile. 'Not tonight.' She turned and opened the door. She was out of the car before he had reacted and almost running away across the pavement. As she fumbled with her key she heard the car shoot away, exhaust roaring. Her body went limp and she leaned on the door, shuddering. Tears stung behind her closed eyes.

CHAPTER NINE

LAURA rang her father's secretary early next morning. 'Has my father heard these rumours?' she asked point blank, and the woman sighed.

'Not yet. I've been talking to the hospital. He's going to have his operation tomorrow and he's in total isolation—no newspapers, no radio or television, no visitors. There's no way he can hear about what's going on—and his doctor insists that it's vital he has the operation, whatever's happening to the company.'

'Have you discussed it with my brother? Does Philip know the truth, now?'

'Yes.' Miss Harris was oddly guarded, her tone clipped.

'You told him yesterday? Was he shocked?'

Miss Harris paused. 'I think the news of his father's illness seriously alarmed him.'

Laura wasn't sure if she was imagining it, but she was picking up some unspoken comment, a hidden feeling which Miss Harris was carefully suppressing.

'What's he doing about the City?'

Miss Harris said flatly: 'I've no idea. You would have to discuss that with him. I only hope Mr Sloane doesn't hold me responsible.'

Laura frowned. 'How did the rumours start, then?' Had Miss Harris been indiscreet? Of course, that was obvious. She must have said something to somebody and within a short time the news would have flashed all round the City.

Miss Harris wasn't admitting anything. 'I couldn't say,' she said, rather stiffly, and made a polite excuse to ring off.

George Sloane was going to be very angry with her when he realised what had happened. Laura was sorry for Miss Harris. She wouldn't like to be in her shoes. If her father survived his operation he would murder his secretary when he found out what she had done.

Picking up the phone again, Laura rang Philip. His secretary said in a flustered voice that he wasn't available. Hiding under the table, Laura recognised. Philip would be running scared. He wouldn't have a clue how to cope with the situation.

'Tell him I urgently need to speak to him,' she told the girl.

'I'll give him your message,' she was promised, but Laura suspected Philip wouldn't be ringing back. He would be too busy finding a hole big enough to conceal him from the rest of the world.

There seemed to be nothing she could do. Philip wouldn't know what to do. Her father could not be told. Simon was going to buy up every share he could at the lowest price he could risk and within a very short time he might well have enough shares to hold a pistol to the head of the Sloane board. Laura sat down and worked it out. She was sufficiently aware of the way companies worked to realise that Simon would force her father's board to give him a seat on it, and once he was a director he would have no difficulty managing Philip. This was the first crisis her brother had had to face alone and he had just gone to pieces. Simon would have a walkover.

Simon knew far too much about the Sloane company. He probably knew all the directors extremely well and he would have a shrewd idea which of them he could twist to his own purpose.

Even if her father survived his operation he was going to find his world very different when he was fit enough to return to work.

Yes, Laura thought grimly, Miss Harris had a lot to answer for! And if she knew her father, the reckoning would come once he was up on his feet again.

Last night Laura had been sick with misery over Simon, but she had got up this morning in a fighting mood and she was determined not to let herself lose her common sense again. Simon had made no secret of the fact that he was determined to pursue a vendetta against her family. His passionate lovemaking had confused her briefly into believing he meant it, but in the cold light of morning she had realised how dangerous it would be to believe a word he said or a thing he did. She wasn't going to let him use her as a weapon against her father. He had tried to use Annette. Her father had seen immediately that that was his reason for pursuing Annette and he had been a hundred per cent right. Having failed with Annette he had turned his attention to Laura.

He wasn't going to succeed with her, either, she determined. She was going to clamp down on every sign of attraction inside herself. Last night had been madness, and she wouldn't repeat it.

She felt so helpless sitting here, not having a clue how to act, knowing that Simon would be engaged in taking over her father's company yet not knowing how to stop him.

Suddenly she thought of Donald and leapt to the phone. A moment later she was talking to him and getting a picture of worried indecision. 'It's all most unfortunate. I've been talking to Philip. I've offered to help as far as I can, but I've no authority to act without agreement. I can't buy in Sloane shares without being absolutely certain I'm well covered. The trouble is, Hilliard will have a head start on me. By the time I've talked to our people he may well have achieved his objectives.'

'He's buying already?' Laura asked, her heart sinking.

'I can't say for certain, but prices dropped the moment the market opened and then picked up—which suggests someone was waiting to buy. I think we can be pretty sure that was Hilliard. If he goes on buying the price will stabilise and perhaps even rise. But it will be too late to do anything to stop him.'

'Have you any idea what Philip is doing?' Laura asked. 'I couldn't get hold of him this morning.'

Donald paused. 'He was worried,' he said cagily.

Donald might be a slightly comic figure in his private life, but on his own ground he was mildly impressive. He knew precisely what he was doing as far as money was concerned.

'I should damned well hope he was worried!' Laura exploded. 'Father will slay him alive!'

'I'm afraid he won't be pleased,' Donald agreed.

'Did Philip know how the rumour got out?'

'What?' Donald sounded odd.

'Did he say anything about it?' Laura asked sharply.

'Er . . .' Donald mumbled.

'What did he say?'

'Don't think too badly of him, Laura,' Donald sighed with obvious unhappiness. 'I'm sorry for him.'

Laura's fingers tightened round the phone. 'Are you

saying it was Philip?'

'He realises he made a mistake,' Donald said. 'He's pretty sick about it.'

'Philip started the rumours?' Laura closed her eyes. 'Oh, no, how could he be so stupid? What happened?'

'He had a crisis in one of the factories—an explosion wrecked the plant and someone was killed. Philip naturally wanted to speak to your father at once. Miss Harris told him that was impossible and told him to deal with the situation himself.' Donald gave another long sigh. 'Philip was thrown into a sort of panic, I'm afraid. He was having lunch with an old school friend and he talked too much.'

'Oh, no!' Laura exclaimed. 'Didn't he realise what he was doing?'

'I don't think he did,' Donald told her. 'After all, an old friend! Philip didn't suspect the man would repeat what he'd said.'

'Then he must be crazy!'

Donald neither agreed nor disagreed. 'Of course, when the rumours started Miss Harris told him the truth, but . . .'

'It was too late,' Laura said drily.

'I'm afraid so. The damage was done.'

'And now Philip is scared out of his wits about what Father is going to say?'

'He's very worried,' Donald agreed. 'What do you think your father's chances are, Laura? I told Annette and she was very upset, of course. She wanted to go and see him, but the hospital isn't allowing any visitors.'

'Father said fifty-fifty and we must hope he was right. There's one thing—if determination has anything to do with it, he'll make it. I can't see him giving up without a struggle.'

'No,' said Donald, 'that's what I told Annette. If you had time could you drop in and comfort her? She keeps crying.'

'I'll go and see her,' Laura agreed, and then rang off.

Annette was pale and tear-stained. She gave Laura a damp-eyed look and wailed: 'He's going to die—I know he's going to die! I can't bear it!'

'He's far too tough to die without a fight,' Laura told her, thinking it was just as well the hospital wasn't allowing visitors, because if anything could depress someone about to have a serious operation it was listening to someone else weeping that they were going to die.

'I'm so worried,' Annette wept. 'And just when I was planning my wedding. It isn't fair!'

Eyeing her wryly, Laura pointed out that it was months before the wedding date. 'Father will be up and about again by then.'

'If he lives,' Annette said with a gulp. 'Why do things happen? I was having a wonderful time and now I'm miserable.'

'Never mind,' said Laura, patting her shoulder. 'Shall I make you some coffee?'

'I'll have a drink,' Annette decided. 'I need something to cheer me up. I'm very fond of Father, you know I am. I couldn't bear it if anything happened to him. Why didn't he tell me? Why did he keep it a secret?'

'He didn't want you worried,' Laura soothed.

'Oh, he's so good to me,' Annette groaned. 'What are we going to do? How soon will we know if he's going to be all right?'

'It will be a few days,' Laura told her. 'A week or possibly two, I imagine. It's a very serious operation, Annette.'

She shouldn't have said that—it started Annette off again on a noisy crying jag. When she could be talked out of that she went off to the bathroom to wash her face and restore it to its usual ravishing state. Conversation had never been easy with Annette, whose topics of discussion were strictly limited to herself and her concerns, but under present circumstances they became impossible. She did not feel she could talk about her wedding or any happier subject and any mention of their father made her tears start up again. Laura was quite relieved to get away.

She rang Miss Harris again that afternoon. Warily the secretary admitted that there had been heavy selling and buying on the market. The facts about George Sloane's illness were now common knowledge, but it had not calmed the City. He was far too important to his company. His removal from the scene left a power vacuum inside the Sloane company and nobody seriously imagined Philip could fill it.

'Is it known who's buying?' Laura asked, without mentioning Simon.

Miss Harris said it was not known, but her tone suggested she had a very good idea.

'What are the board doing?' Laura enquired.

'Talking,' Miss Harris said with a dry note in her voice.

Laura rang off and walked to the window. Talking, she thought. That would do a lot of good. Simon would have no trouble at all with that collection of stuffed dummies. George Sloane had been very careful to collect a crowd of yes-men around him, but he had left out of his calculations the probability that men who say yes to one person will say yes to another if the incentive is strong enough.

There was no point in pretending to work. Her mind was in no fit state to concentrate on anything. She rang the hospital and was told that her father was perfectly well and would definitely be having his operation on the following morning. It would be over, she was told, by lunchtime.

The afternoon dragged into evening. Laura listened to music and tried not to dwell too much on her father. In an odd way it seemed far more painful to her because of the icy gulf between them. The normal human reactions of someone whose father is dangerously close to death were denied to her. Annette was going through the whole thing far more easily. She could cry and protest her unhappiness. Annette acted so much of her life. She went through the motions, doing what instinct told her was expected of her at this moment. Since she rarely thought of anything except as it affected her, she seemed to see her relationship with her father in a totally different light from the way Laura saw her own. George Sloane had always given Annette more attention than he had given either Philip or Laura. Laura wondered if that was because Annette's insincerity made it easier for him to pretend to be a normal father. Annette had never demanded more of him than he was prepared to give. He had showered her with valuable gifts and both of them had seen that as a sign of love. Annette had been more than content with the charade they played out in public.

Laura could not find a role of that sort for herself. From her childhood upward she had questioned her father's behaviour both to her and to her mother.

Aware of his cold, selfish ruthlessness, she had never tried to learn any more about him. There was no residue of affection for her to call on now. She had no idea what it was she felt. In times of personal crisis we always fall back on our idea of how we should behave, how we should feel, even when our feelings are instinctively taking that very path. The outward form of behaviour corresponds to society's belief in conventional patterns of action. The inner emotions usually mirror them. But when the inner emotion is lacking it is very hard to perform the rites society demands of us. We look for a response in ourselves to every major event of life from the death of someone in our family to the birth of a child, and we are always disturbed when the instinctive reaction does not match what we know is expected of us.

Laura went to bed late that night, torn emotionally between a sense of guilt and the constant memory of a relationship which could not produce any emotion stronger than regret.

Annette arrived next morning and demanded company. 'I can't be alone all day today,' she said.

'Have you taken the day off? Was that a good idea? Wouldn't it be easier to work and keep your mind off Father?'

Annette looked horrified. 'How can you be so callous? How could I work when he might die today?'

Laura had intended to work. She knew she would be struggling all the time to keep her mind on what she was doing, but she also knew that if she sat around talking to Annette she might go out of her mind. There was nothing for them to talk about. In other circumstances they might have talked about their childhood, swapped memories of their father, laughed about old family jokes. But the Sloanes had no such happy memories of their father. He had rarely been at home and when he had he had kept them all at a distance.

Annette drank black coffee and complained about Donald's mother. 'She's ruining the wedding plans. She keeps coming up with lists of boring relatives who live in Land's End or John o' Groats and have never so much as seen Donald but must be invited. And she wants me to live with them—says I'm not old enough to run a house of my own.'

Wise lady, Laura thought, imagining how Annette would run a home. If her flat was anything to go by, Donald would be very uncomfortable if Annette was in charge of their home.

'I'm not living with that old crow,' Annette announced. 'She can think again. Donald will do what I want, not what she wants.'

That was probably true. Annette had enormous energy. She would make short work of both Donald and his mother.

'Don't antagonise Mrs Foulds,' Laura advised, looking at her sister soberly. 'She could make life very difficult for you.'

'She'd better not try!' Annette sounded vicious, her face childishly irritated.

Laura shrugged. Her eye caught the clock. 'I think I'll ring the hospital,' she said, getting up. 'The operation should be over by now.'

Annette followed her to the phone and hovered, watching her. Laura got through to the ward Sister to whom she had spoken several times already. 'Yes,' she was told, 'it's over. Your father is back in his own bed.'

'He's all right?' Laura hardly dared to ask the question. She just did not know how she was going to feel if the answer was in the negative.

'He's come through quite nicely,' the Sister said coolly. 'We'll let you know if anything changes.'

Laura put the phone down, and Annette burst out with anxious questions. 'Is everything okay? Is he going to be all right? What did they say?'

'So far, so good,' Laura soothed. 'I suppose we won't know very much until they finally let us visit him, but at least he's got through the operation safely.'

'I knew he would,' said Annette, sparkling. 'I told you. Father's too tough to let a little thing like an operation worry him.' She picked up the phone. 'I'll ring Donald and give him the good news.'

Laura watched her as she talked excitedly, her face vivacious. 'Yes, that would be great,' she said, laughing. 'Will you meet us there? Fine, see you.' She put the phone down and grinned at Laura. 'Donald's delighted. He and Philip are meeting us for lunch. Philip was with him, so Donald suggested we all have lunch.'

'Now?' Laura gave her an impatient glance. 'There isn't time to get ready.'

'You look fine,' Annette assured her, secure in her own dazzling appearance. 'Oh, come on, don't fuss, Laura. A family lunch—isn't that a good idea?' Her smile went. 'As long as Philip doesn't drag that awful Daphne along too.'

Philip and Donald were on their own when the two girls arrived, however, to Annette's unhidden delight. Laura noticed that Philip was looking worried and pale. While Annette was burbling to Donald, Laura drew her brother aside and asked how the run on the shares was going. 'Have prices steadied?'

Philip gave her a gloomy, shifty look. 'Donald told you all about it, I suppose? Father's going to be furious with me. How was I to know? He didn't take me into his confidence. He told his secretary, but he didn't tell me. He can't blame me if I was worried. But he will, of course. He'll put all the blame at my door, and that's not fair. I meant well. How was I to know Ted would blab it all round the city?'

'What are you and the board doing about it?' Laura asked, avoiding the subject of blame.

Philip gave a heavy sigh. 'Waiting to see what will happen. We've been in contact with everyone who has a big holding to reassure them, but some of them had sold already.'

'To Simon Hilliard?'

Philip turned a dark red. 'Yes,' he muttered. 'We don't know yet how much he's got hold of, but Father isn't going to like it.'

They all moved into the restaurant to begin their meal, talking, a peculiar mixture of gloom and relief hanging over them. George Sloane had pulled through his operation triumphantly, but if he continued to hold his own and finally emerged from hospital to return to work, he was going to tear his son into little strips. Donald looked at Philip with compunction.

'Would it help if I talked to your father before he heard from anyone else?'

'I doubt if anything will help,' Philip said in a hangdog voice. 'I'm going to get slaughtered.'

'You're an idiot,' Annette told him. 'Serves you right!'

'Thanks,' Philip muttered. He sat back, scowling, and his eye moved round the restaurant. Laura heard him take a sudden sharp breath. She glanced in the direction he had been looking in and saw Simon, the shock of it making her own breath stop for a beat of time. Hurriedly she looked away, but not before she had seen the woman with him and wondered jealously who it was. She hadn't seen her before. She was slim, elegant, a dark-haired woman with a smooth pale complexion and tranquil blue eyes. Laura gave her one look which took in everything about her, including the fact that at that moment her hand was resting on Simon's arm and she was smiling at him in an intimate, gentle way which indicated a relationship of some depth.

Annette hadn't noticed them. She was talking to Donald about flats. 'I want to live in London, and a flat would be easier to run than a house.'

'But, Annette——' Donald began, and she did not let him finish.

'I'm not going to live with your mother! It never works to live with in-laws, does it, Laura?'

'Don't drag me into it!'

'You know I'm right! You wouldn't, would you? Everyone says it doesn't work. It only leads to rows. I want my own home.'

'Why not a house?' Donald asked glumly, watching the waiter pouring wine into his glass.

'I like flats—much easier to run.' Annette ran a hand into her vivid flame-like hair. 'I'm not giving up my job, you know. I like working there. I'm not turning into a vegetable. We can get one of those service flats and have no problems to worry about. All the domestic work is done for you, you know.'

Donald's shoulders hunched. He drank some wine, staring at the bowl of flowers in the centre of the table. Laura was sorry for him, but he had been desperate to

marry Annette. He had made his bed—quite literally.
Now he was going to have to lie on it.

Annette was fiercely determined to win her struggle
with Donald's mother. It engrossed far more of her
attention than Donald himself. Her face took on a vicious look whenever she mentioned Mrs Foulds. Laura
shuddered to visualise Donald's future with both
women fighting over him like cats.

During the lunch she switched off her attention,
fixing a vague smile to her face which the others took
for a sign of interest, hardly aware of the running
argument between Annette and Donald, the glum
remarks Philip made now and then. She couldn't have
said what she was eating. The food went into her
mouth without her eye ever noticing it.

The only thing that she was aware of was Simon and
his companion. She didn't look directly towards them.
After that first brief glance she had resolutely kept her
eyes away from them. But she was aware of them every
second of the time, her lashes lowered and her eyes
noting each small shift of their bodies, each inflection of
their low voices, each smile the woman gave to Simon as
he talked to her.

Laura could pick up a certain gravity in whatever
they were discussing. Simon wasn't smiling. His usual
vivacity was absent. He was doing most of the talking,
leaning towards his companion. Several times the
woman reached across the table and touched his hand.

Laura managed to take a long, furtive inspection of
the green dress the woman wore, the tiny ear-studs
glinting as the dark head turned, the curve of the other
woman's slim figure. She picked up each detail in a
rapid flick of her eyes which did not stop in case either
of them noticed Laura looking that way. She had to

admire the woman's taste. And she disliked her intensely, her nape prickling with hostility every time her ears picked up the soft warm voice.

She felt them both standing up, realised they were leaving. Annette gave a little gasp. 'There's Simon! Simon! Hi, Simon!'

Oh, God, Laura thought bitterly, does she have to? Annette was waving her hand, beaming. Laura prayed that Simon would ignore her. She didn't think she could stand having that woman standing beside the table. She already felt sick at the idea of any closer contact.

She heard Simon say coolly: 'Hallo, Annette.' His voice was no closer. Laura looked through her lowered lashes and saw him walking away.

'Well, really,' Annette said discontentedly. 'He might have come over. Who's that with him? Not exactly a raving beauty, is she? Thirty if she's a day.'

Laura drew a long, harsh breath. For a moment she had thought Simon was going to come over and she had been sick at the idea. Now she was sick because he hadn't, he had just walked indifferently away.

'Coffee, sir?' The waiter was stooping over Philip, who gave a start and reddened.

'Oh—er—yes, thanks.'

Laura looked up and met her brother's miserable eyes. Poor Philip, life was just too difficult for him. It wasn't his fault that he had not inherited the cold brain and ruthless confidence of his father. He was looking like someone who wishes they had enough nerve to cut their own throat. Laura smiled at him wryly.

'Cheer up, it may never happen.'

'It already has,' Philip muttered.

CHAPTER TEN

LAURA left the others at three o'clock and went back to her flat. It seemed quiet and empty and remarkably peaceful after the long, boring lunch she had had to endure. Before she started work she rang the hospital again and was told her father was still under the influence of the anaesthetic. 'He won't be round until tonight, but don't worry. If anything happened we'd let you know.'

Laura rang off and went to her little studio. The light streamed into the bare room. She sat down and stared at the unfinished painting; and the round dark eyes of the bird stared back at her. She realised she was sick of the book. She seemed to have been working on it for ever. The sooner it was finished the better she would like it.

The tedious, painstaking work suited her mood today, though. It forced her to concentrate on each delicate brush-stroke. She bent her head, shutting out everything else, her hand deft as she worked.

At seven the light was less suitable for work. The sky had clouded over. A thin veil had been drawn over the skyline, promising rain, the air scented with it. Laura went to the window and opened it, leaned out to inhale. A chaffinch was sitting on a branch nearby, the bright dark eye watching her curiously as though it was waiting for crumbs.

'Hang on,' she told it, beginning to smile. She went into the kitchen and found some bread. When she got back and sprinkled crumbs along the windowsill she shut the window and stood back to watch the birds arriving. After a moment several belligerent pigeons chased the smaller birds away and made short work of the crumbs. Laura laughed as she watched them strutting to and fro, looking at her through the glass in expectation. 'Oh, no, you don't,' she told them. 'You've had enough.'

The doorbell rang suddenly, making her jump. She looked at her watch, her face disturbed. Her father? Was something wrong? She rushed to the door, half expecting to find Philip or Donald there, but when she pulled it open she saw Simon standing there, his face pale and harsh.

'Oh.' She couldn't think of a thing to say, staring up at him in breathless alarm.

'I've got to talk to you.'

She came out of shock, stiffening. 'I don't want to talk to you.'

'I don't care what you want. You have to listen.' He spoke the words roughly, his voice uneven.

Laura began to close the door, her hand trembling, but Simon pushed it open again and forced his way past her into the flat.

'Get out!' she flung at him, wishing she could stop the helpless shaking which had invaded her body.

'Not until I've said what I came to say.' He walked down the corridor towards her sitting-room and she followed him, staring at the back of the black head with bitter hostility.

He turned, his hands in his pockets, his heavy lids veiling his eyes. 'I wanted to tell you this the other night, but I couldn't do that without asking someone's permission to break my promise not to talk about it.'

'If it's that secret perhaps you'd better not tell me anything,' Laura muttered. 'You shouldn't be here. My father is very ill and you're doing your best to destroy him. I don't want you here!'

'Just listen,' Simon said curtly. He gestured with one hand. 'Sit down.'

'Now, look . . .'

'Sit down, for God's sake!' he broke out hoarsely, his lids lifting to show her the green eyes full of that deep, angry glow which she had come to recognise.

Laura would have gone on arguing, but she was disturbed by the expression in those eyes. She meekly sat down on the couch and Simon stood in front of her, staring at her bent head.

'I'll start way back,' he said brusquely. 'With my sister. She was eighteen and she got a job at Sloane's. I got it for her, in fact. She and I are alone in the world. Our parents are dead. Ginny was the only person who mattered a damn to me, so I wanted her where I could keep an eye on her. She was very pretty and I knew enough about my own sex to want to keep her out of trouble. Phil and I were friends then. We often went out together. We were much of an age and we had a few things in common. I trusted him. It never occurred to me that Phil, of all people, might make a pass at Ginny. He didn't seem the type.'

Laura sat listening, staring at her hands, beginning to feel cold. Her mind went leaping ahead of what Simon was saying, guessing what was to come, and shivering at the realisation of what it meant.

'To do him justice, he was in love with her then. And Ginny was crazy about him. She was only eighteen, remember, and Philip seemed a man of the world to her. He was the boss's son and not bad looking. He took her around in a fancy car and spent money on her like water, and Ginny fell like a ton of bricks.'

'I don't think you should be telling me this,' Laura whispered, her teeth tight. She didn't want to hear any more.

'I've got to,'. Simon burst out. 'There isn't much more. The first I knew about it was when Ginny took an overdose and ended up in a hospital having her insides pumped out.'

Laura drew a painful breath. 'Oh, no!'

'Oh, yes. She'd got pregnant and naturally ran to Philip to tell him, expecting him to marry her at once. Instead he rushed to your father and your father calmly told Ginny to have an abortion. He told her Philip wasn't marrying her—no way. She wasn't on the list of eligible young ladies who would make a suitable match for George Sloane's son. Instead of standing up to him Ginny went home and took some pills. What hurt her most wasn't your father's attitude, it was that Philip didn't even try to stand up to his father. He just stood there looking miserable.'

'What happened to her?' Laura asked faintly, feeling pretty sick herself.

'She lost the baby—naturally. She was ill for quite a while after that. When she was better she got another job elsewhere. So did I. After I'd told your father what I thought of him and his precious son.'

'So that's why you walked out?'

He nodded grimly. 'I'd been planning to start up on my own, anyway, but that precipitated things. I was angry enough to kill your father the night I went along to see him after I'd seen my sister. She'd looked like death and she was so damned young. If she'd told me, I'd have moved heaven and earth to make Phil marry her.'

'She wouldn't have wanted that,' Laura said wryly.

Simon shot her a hard look. 'No, she said that herself. She said she would have rather jumped off the top of the Post Office Tower than have Philip forced to marry her when he obviously didn't want to.'

'I'm sorry,' Laura murmured with guilty anguish. 'I wish I'd known. What can I say that isn't inadequate?'

Simon shrugged, moving away. With his back to her he said, 'It worked out for her in the end. She married a very nice man and has got two lovely kids. But I never forgot what the Sloanes had done to her, and I told myself that one day I'd get my own back. I've been on my way to destroying your father for years, working like a slave to get my own business off the ground and getting myself into a position where I could really take him on.'

Laura couldn't find it in herself to blame him for his desire for revenge, having heard the story about his sister.

'Then I met you,' Simon muttered.

Laura's body jerked with pain. She looked at the back of his bent head, her face white.

He swung round, his face haggard, and looked at her across the room. 'It's a mess,' he muttered, his voice low and tormented. 'I've told myself over and over again not to be a fool. You're a Sloane, and I can't be crazy enough to feel like this about a Sloane. I haven't slept properly for a week, agonising over it.'

Laura's fingers clutched at each other so tightly it hurt. The blood stopped flowing in them, they began to turn white. She tried to regularise her breathing, but each breath was drawn with jerky rapidity, sounding so loud in her own ears that she was afraid he must hear.

'I can't be in love with you,' Simon said in a husky

voice. 'Not now, not when your damned father is right in the palm of my hand and I can crush him like an old eggshell whenever I choose to do so.' His hand opened and closed in the air with violence. 'I've got him—exactly where I want him. Exactly the way I always planned. He can't do a thing to stop me, that's the beauty of it. Philip's a cipher, always has been, always will be. Sloane's is right in my grasp and everything is working like magic.'

'You've bought enough shares?' she asked in a thin dry, little voice, staring at him.

'More than enough to force them to give me a seat on the board. Your father is going to be out of action for months after this operation, even if he survives it. And if he does ever come back, he'll find me running Sloane's.'

'Well, I hope that you're satisfied,' said Laura, her mind having worked the whole problem out. It might help a little to realise that Simon had had a struggle before he finally decided to wreak his planned revenge, but he had done it. Whatever he felt for her hadn't stopped him.

'Satisfied?' Simon flung the word back at her harshly. 'What do you think I've been going through for the last few days? I've been setting the wheels in motion, pretending to myself that nothing had changed, that I was going to destroy your father just the way I planned years ago.' His mouth writhed in a pale grimace, his wide shoulders stiffly set.

'Aren't you?' Laura asked him flatly. 'You bought the shares.'

'Oh, I went through the charade. I kept telling myself you were a Sloane, a damned Sloane.' He ran his fingers through his hair, leaving it dishevelled and wild. 'But I don't damned well care,' he groaned. 'I only care about one thing now.' His eyes flashed across the room, their dark pupils enormous, then he was striding towards her, pulling her up and into his arms. Laura gave a startled gasp before his hard mouth crushed down against her lips and he kissed her with a bitter, burning passion which had no softness in it.

She pushed against his shoulders without avail. Simon wouldn't release her, wouldn't let her escape the fierce possession of his kiss, bending her back in his arms to insist that she accept and finally return with smothered weakness the passion which was unleashed between them.

When he finally lifted his head her lips were hot and bruised, her heart pounding violently inside her chest.

'I'm in love with you,' Simon muttered.

She swayed forward and put her head on his shoulder, trembling. 'Simon,' she whispered.

He covered her head with one hand, pressing her face into him. 'Tell me you love me.' His voice was oddly uncertain, shaking.

'Yes,' she said into his shoulder, 'I love you.'

For a moment they just stood there, pressing together, the piercing sweetness of declared love binding them together in a silence which was half pain, half pleasure.

Laura lifted her head. 'But we're never going to be happy,' she said miserably. 'How could we be? There's too much to come between us, Simon.'

'I've told myself that a thousand times. That's why I had to see my sister, talk to her and explain how I felt about you. That was her with me at lunch.'

'Oh,' said Laura, all her hostility towards the dark-haired woman vanishing. 'That was your sister? She looked very charming.'

'Ginny's a darling. She understood. She told me to be happy and said she'd forgiven Philip years ago. She realises now that she would never have been as happy with him as she has been with the fellow she did marry. Her marriage works perfectly and she adores her kids. She said she has no ill will towards Philip.' He grimaced. 'I'll admit she isn't crazy about your father, but, as she said, I'm not marrying George Sloane.'

Laura looked at him uncertainly. 'Simon, if you take over the company it's going to make tremendous ill-will between you and my father.'

'And that's going to wreck our chances of a happy marriage?' He gave her a wry little smile. 'I know. I'm going to have to grin and bear being George Sloane's son-in-law. I shan't like it, but I shall put up with it if I have to—to get you I'd put up with having the devil himself as my father-in-law.'

Laura trembled. 'You won't press to get control?'

He shook his head. 'I shan't go any further with my plans. I'm not going to start my marriage by chopping off your father's head.'

Her relief was so great she swayed, her eyes enormous. 'Thank you, Simon.'

He touched her cheek with one hand gently, his eyes caressing her. 'You'll marry me?'

'Yes,' she said, smiling, her heart turning over.

'Oh, darling,' he muttered, bending his head to kiss her again. They clung to each other, kissing desperately. Laura had been so certain that Simon was lost to her, after hearing about his sister's experience with Philip and their father, that she was unable to believe that after all things were not totally hopeless. As his mouth moved demandingly against her own she was melting closer to him, her pulses racing.

'I'm so sorry about your sister,' she said later, as they sat in each other's arms on the couch.

'She had a rough deal,' he agreed.

'I'm ashamed of Philip.'

'He's a spineless jellyfish,' Simon nodded.

'And my father ...' Laura halted, unable to say what she thought of her father's behaviour.

'A swine,' Simon said curtly. 'I'm sorry you had to hear about it. It didn't make a pretty story.'

'It didn't surprise me. My father isn't an angel. He made my mother very unhappy.' She began to tell him about her mother and Simon listened, his face intent.

'I wondered where you got it from,' he said.

Laura smiled, her eyes amused. 'Not from my father,' she accepted.

'No,' Simon agreed. 'Not from him.'

'You did mean to seduce Annette just to annoy my father, didn't you?' she asked, fixing him with her wide, intelligent blue eyes.

He looked down into them, his face wry. 'Confession time?'

'Why not? I already guessed.'

'Annette was willing and she made it a very enjoyable prospect,' he said with a wicked grin. 'I knew it would scare your father out of his wits to wonder if I could talk her into marrying me. Quite apart from his fury if I did seduce her, there was also that threat that she might bring me into the firm as his son-in-law. Annette handed me a very tempting weapon and I meant to make full use of it.' He gave her a slanting teasing smile. 'As I said, until I met you.'

'And you thought you might add another tempting weapon to your armoury, did you?' she mocked.

He laughed. 'The thought did cross my mind, especially after I'd realised to my surprise that I really fancied you a lot more than I fancied Annette. She's a sexy little bitch, but she's got the brains of a flea.'

'Not very kind,' Laura said, shaking her head.

'But true,' he told her drily. 'You had brains and a sense of humour and you turned me on the minute I set eyes on you. It was a bit of a shock to find you were a Sloane, in fact.'

'That did occur to me,' Laura agreed. 'Your face changed so drastically once you knew who I was.'

'If I'd had any sense I'd have steered clear of you after that party,' Simon mused. 'When I saw you again in the Zoo that day I knew I'd been dying to see you ever since that night. And after you'd spiked my guns with Annette I was annoyed with you and wanted to make you admit you fancied me.' He grinned at her. 'Because I knew damned well you did.'

'Oh, you knew, did you?'

His green eyes gleamed. 'Admit it. You fancied me as much as I fancied you right from the start.'

'I'm admitting nothing,' Laura said softly, looking demurely at him.

'Typical woman,' he commented.

'Don't generalise. I'm neither a typical woman nor a typical Sloane,' said Laura. 'I'm me.'

'And delightful with it,' Simon grinned, brushing her neck with his lips and making her skin tingle with pleasure.

'My father isn't going to like it,' Laura thought aloud.

'He'll have to put up with it,' Simon shrugged. 'I expect the blow will be softened by the fact that I've bought all those Sloane shares. At least our marriage will keep them in the family.'

Laura began to laugh. 'Give him a few weeks and he'll think he planned it!'

Simon grinned. 'I wouldn't mind betting that's just what he will believe.'

'Annette will be livid,' Laura said dreamily, the thought not displeasing to her. Annette was going to swell up with rage, like a balloon, and explode all over the place. She was going to be convinced that Laura planned this long ago.

Simon looked down at her, mockery in his smile. 'That seems to leave you quite unafraid,' he said in dry appreciation. His eyes sharpened. 'What about this Declan?'

'Oh, Declan,' shrugged Laura, trying not to laugh.

'Yes, Declan,' Simon said, his hand curving round her throat. 'I never really believed he meant a thing, but you used him ruthlessly to drive me crazy, didn't you? I was never quite certain whether he was a red herring or not, and that's what you intended, you tormenting little madam.'

Laura's blue eyes gleamed up at him. 'Sorry,' she said, smiling. 'Declan is my publisher, full stop. Nothing more.'

'I thought as much,' said Simon, his smile full of satisfaction. 'When we're married you can change your publisher, though.'

'I can't do that,' Laura said, horrified. 'Poor Declan! And then there's Henry and the bats—I was looking forward to working on that book.'

'From now on you're going to concentrate on me,' Simon told her in firm tones.

'Oh, no,' Laura informed him. 'I enjoy my career.'

'I know something you'll enjoy just as much,' Simon said with a restless movement, pulling her towards him.

'Now listen——' she began, and got no further.

She would have made a more determined protest if she could have got free, but Simon held her far too tightly and kissed her far too hard. She abandoned the struggle after a token little wriggle and wound her arms around his neck. They could discuss the rest later, she thought, submitting eagerly.

What readers say about Harlequin Presents

"Harlequin books are so refreshing that they take you into a different world with each one you read."

D.L.,* Jacksboro, Texas

"I hope Harlequin goes on forever."

M.Z., Hollywood, California

"Harlequin books are great; once you start reading them, you always want to read more."

T.E., Ogden, Utah

"Harlequin books bring love, happiness and romance into my very routine life."

N.J., Springfield, Missouri

*Names available on request

Take these
4 best-selling novels
FREE

That's right! FOUR first-rate Harlequin romance novels by four world renowned authors, FREE, as your introduction to the Harlequin Presents Subscription Plan. Be swept along by these FOUR exciting, poignant and sophisticated novels . . . Travel to the Mediterranean island of Cyprus in **Anne Hampson**'s "Gates of Steel" . . . to Portugal for **Anne Mather**'s "Sweet Revenge" . . . to France and **Violet Winspear**'s "Devil in a Silver Room" . . . and the sprawling state of Texas for **Janet Dailey**'s "No Quarter Asked."

Harlequin Presents...

The very finest in romantic fiction

Join the millions of avid Harlequin readers all over the world who delight in the magic of a really exciting novel. SIX great NEW titles published EACH MONTH! Each month you will get to know exciting, interesting, true-to-life people . . . . You'll be swept to distant lands you've dreamed of visiting . . . . Intrigue, adventure, romance, and the destiny of many lives will thrill you through each Harlequin Presents novel.

Get all the latest books before they're sold out!
As a Harlequin subscriber you actually receive your personal copies of the latest Presents novels immediately after they come off the press, so you're sure of getting all 6 each month.

Cancel your subscription whenever you wish!
You don't have to buy any minimum number of books. Whenever you decide to stop your subscription just let us know and we'll cancel all further shipments.

Your FREE gift includes

Sweet Revenge by **Anne Mather**
Devil in a Silver Room by **Violet Winspear**
Gates of Steel by **Anne Hampson**
No Quarter Asked by **Janet Dailey**